Acknowledgements
Davey Robb the youngest Royal Marine to serve in
42 Commando in the Falklands conflict in 1982. For all his help in
getting the facts correct in the writing of this book

Thanks to Bob Gair for his help in proof reading and editing

Thanks to my wife for designing the cover for this book

PREFACE

Tug Wilson ex-Royal Marine part-time singer in a C&W band author of mushy romance novels

Medically discharged from 42 Commando Royal Marines after being seriously wounded and witnessing the death of his best friend in the Falklands war.

While recovering from his wounds in hospital Tug Suffers from betrayal from an unfaithful wife. Encouraged by his sister Jean, Tug takes up writing becoming a successful novelist always looking for new scenarios for his next story

Whist doing a Good Samaritan deed, Tug stops to help a stranded woman and fix a punctured tyre on her car. The woman who he recognised as that posh girl from his school days who they both shared a mutual contempt for each other.

She is going through marital problems. Tug decides to help her. But with the ulterior motive of using her story as a scenario for one of his novels. As he becomes more involved, he discovers there is a fine line between love and hate

PROUD MARY

Tug, 'Handy you dropped by mate, I need a little favour!" my old Marine comrade Pete said, as I killed Bonnie's engine. Pete hadn't even given me time to kick the prop-stand down, let alone climb off the bike.

Bonnie, by the way, is my 1962 vintage Triumph Bonneville. She's probably a little old-fashioned when compared to modern bikes, but she's the real deal, something I'd dreamed of owning since I'd first clapped eyes on one as a young man. By then I had enough money to indulge my whims; I'd picked her up at an auction some years before, just after my divorce. Almost a derelict, I'd had Pete and his boys completely rebuild her.

I'd been out on the bike theoretically blowing the cobwebs out of my mind, after spending most of the night sitting in front of the computer screen. I'd hoped the ride out might give me some time to think before I got down to work, yet again. Well, the ride would have blown the cobwebs away, if it weren't for the bloody skid lid law.

As I recall, I hadn't been in the mood for writing anymore that morning, but I was running tight on the publishing date for my latest masterpiece, so I needed to push myself. To be honest, I doubted spending the night forcing myself to write had done much good for my demeanour that day. And it could probably go some way to explaining some of the things I said and did.

"What's up, Pete?" I asked him.

"Got this bird stuck-out on the A3 London Road somewhere with a flat. I wondered ... well you see, Tug, Steve's out on a job that's going to take him bloody hours. I can't get out to the woman myself, the young lad's out with Dave and other fitter's skiving-off sick today, so I've not got anyone to watch the shop for me. Any chance you might nip out there and change her wheel for me? Otherwise, she'll be waiting all bleedin' day!"

"I'm no fitter, Pete!" I replied. I wasn't trying to talk my way out of the task. My 'oppo' Pete was always doing me favours, so it was an unspoken rule that I'd help him out and he knew it. But experience had taught me not to show too much enthusiasm when it came to handing out such favours.

"Oh come on Tug, you can change a wheel on a Disco as a favour for your favourite old mucker, can't you? Besides that, you never know, you might even get lucky!"

"Pete, I very much suspect that, if she were a tasty piece of stuff," I replied grinning at him, "That you'd be asking me to watch the shop and be on your way out there yourself!"

"Yeah well, I probably would, but her old man's a bit more than I could handle. And besides, Julie would have my guts. Yours too, if she thought you'd covered for me! But, what with you being single and all, you're not in the same boat are you? She is a fair looker mate and to be honest, I can't exactly see her husband calling you out."

"Look, Pete, for your information, I don't go around chasing other people's wives. If they're separated or divorced, well then, maybe I figure they're up for grabs. Otherwise, I steer well clear of the married ones; I ain't no hypocrite, you know!"

"Yeah sorry, I forget about Laura sometimes. Anyway, what about this woman's wheel?"

"Okay, what's her name and vehicle's registration number?"

"Good-on-ya, mate. Mrs Halfon. I haven't got the vehicles registration number off-hand, but it's a Green Discovery. I doubt there's more than one Disco on the London Road with a flat tyre anyway."

"I assume she's got a jack and wheel brace," I asked.

"Yeah, there's a jack in there that I doubt has ever seen the light of day before, and there should be one of those extending wheel braces as well. Put that bugger in there myself, when I sold her old-man the motor."

I kicked Bonnie over to get the old girl started again, and she roared into life. "You owe me, you bugger," I shouted at Pete, as I circled the garage forecourt and took off towards the edge of town.

I'd been conned, yeah I know I had. But as I said, Pete and the boys at the garage had done me enough favours over the years Pete had also saved my life during the Falklands War back in 82.

To be honest, had I just happened to come across the woman I would probably have stopped and offered my assistance anyway; unfortunately that was the kind of clown I was! I just preferred to give folks the impression that I was a bad-boy - it kind of helped to keep most people at arm's length.

After cruising down the High Street - Bonnie's exhaust bumbling away loud enough to let the world know that I was passing - I headed out towards the bypass that would lead me down to the London Road. Winding the old girl-up, once I was out of the built-up area, I enjoyed the exhilaration I always felt when riding her at speed.

About five miles along the London road I spotted the Disco pulled into a lay-by. Its offside front tyre completely flat. Swinging into the lay-by, I passed the Disco and slipped Bonnie on her prop stand in front of the car. Then walked back to the driver's door, unconsciously unzipping my leather jacket as I went. I almost flipped my helmet visor up as well, but for some inexplicable reason, I didn't.

"Mrs Halfon, Pete Brazier from the garage sent me out to change your wheel for you," I said, inspecting the wheel, without really looking at the woman.

"Where's your breakdown lorry?" she demanded, through the half-open window.

I was damned sure that window was down further when I rode past on the bike. By then it was more like three quarters closed. "So Mrs Halfon, is nervous around bikers is she?" was the thought that crossed my mind. Yeah well, I did like to play the part of the ton-up kid, even if I was pushing thirty-six.

All right thirty-seven, but who's counting, it was part of the camouflage.

"No need for the tow truck lady, you've got everything I need in the back of your car. Besides, it's out on another job at the moment and it could be well after lunch before it returns. Pete thought you'd been hanging around here long enough as it was, so he asked me to pop out and change your wheel for you." I replied.

I took a closer look at the woman through my visor and was surprised to find that her face appeared somewhat familiar to me. Something else that I noted, was that quite definitely very recently, she had been crying. It struck me that, if having to hang around and

9

wait for her flat tyre to be changed upset her that much, she should learn how to change the bloody thing herself

A bit of a pity, her doing the old crying bit, that is. She was pretty attractive, except that her make-up was what can only be described as a disaster area. Not the way the elegantly dressed woman normally presented herself in public, I figured.

"Handbrake on?" I asked.

"Yes!" she replied curtly, turning to give me one of those looks. You know, like I'd just questioned her intelligence or something.

For some reason, I found it humorous that she couldn't see my face. I wondered whether that could be the reason for the expression of disdain that she had on her face.

"Yep!" my mind said to me, "you know that face from somewhere!" Then the old brain went into deep retrieval mode trying to place where I have seen the woman before.

Retrieving the jack and wheel brace from the back of the car, I began to undo the spare wheel from its carrier on the rear door. As I did so, I caught sight of the woman in the rearview mirror. Yeah damn it, she was crying again; I could see her dabbing her eyes in the mirror.

Positioning the jack under the car, I raised it a little, until I was sure it was going to have the desired effect; then set about breaking the wheel nuts loose. I think I was on the last but one nut, when I suddenly realised why the woman had looked so familiar and that I could put a name to it that face. Mind you, I'd had to cast my memory back twenty-odd years and the name that I knew her by, wasn't Halfon.

I'd remembered that there were a bunch of so-called "It girls" that went to the same school as I. Most of them were real lookers who - I'd always thought - had a rather inflated opinion of themselves. I figured I'd have some fun, whilst I changed her wheel.

"Right Jan, can you get out of the bloody car now, before I take it up on the jack please?" I shouted at the now fully closed window.

I heard the whine as the window slid down again and Jan's head appeared. "What did you say?"

"Would you get out of the vehicle whilst I jack it up, please? The ground here ain't too clever, and I don't want the jack slipping if you move about at all."

"No, I heard you say that. What did you call me?" She demanded in a somewhat sharp tone of voice.

"Jan, Jan. What did you think I'd call you?" I replied.

"Who told you, that could address me as such?" she demanded.

"Look, you were Janet Symonds the last time I ran into you." I did a quick bit of rethinking "Okay sorry, you're

Janet Halfon now, aren't you! But you didn't change your Christian name did you, Jan." I grinned at her.

To be honest, she gave me a look that I believe I was supposed to wither upon receiving. But I gave that no-never-mind; winding-up posers is one of my favourite pass-times in life. I just grinned back up at her.

"Who are you?" she demanded.

Slowly I reached up, released the strap on my crash helmet and removed it. For a few seconds, Jan stared at me, then an expression of understanding came over her face. But not a very joyous one!

"You're not Ray Tug Wilson, are you?" she asked, still in a demeaning tone of voice.

"Well yeah, but most folks just call me Tug nowadays, Jan."

"Well Mr Tug Wilson, people call me Janet Halfon, or rather Mrs Halfon if they are only acquaintances." she retorted.

I told you I wasn't really in the best of moods that day, so I figured if Janet Halfon was looking for some agro, I was just the guy to give it to her. I wasn't sure what Pete was going to say about me upsetting one of his customers, but I didn't give a shit. After all, I was doing the bitch a favour, wasn't I?

"Yeah well, at the best of times, you always were a stuck-up bitch, Jan. But I never let it bother me at school; so it ain't gonna bother me none now, is it? Now get out of the bleeding motor, please, so's I can change this sodding wheel, will you? Or we're going to be here all bloody night."

"I can see that you're just as arrogant as you were at school, Tug Wilson," Jan said, finally opening the door and getting out of the vehicle. Then she stood there, arm's crossed looking at me with disdain. I had to admit to myself that she still had one killer figure on her, but thought "Shame about the personality!"

But then again, I had her as a captive audience, so I could safely speak my mind

"Get it right, Jan. As I remember things, you and your little clique were stuck-up ignorant bitches. I never looked down on, or bullied any bugger, unlike some folks I know. That includes someone who I could reach with a very short stick, right now."

"How dare you? I've never bullied anyone in my life!" She retorted.

I noted that she didn't deny that she considered few her equal.

"Oh no, what about little Ann Delaney the girl with the funny leg? You and your friends didn't make life too pleasant for her, did you? And then there was Susan Frazier! I seem to recall that you were never too pleasant to her either, just because she carried a bit more weight than most. Mind you, Susan developed quite a figure later on, after she'd lost a few pounds of puppy fat. Put you and all your buddies to shame did our Sue."

"What are you talking about? We never bullied anyone!"

"Yeah well, maybe not in so many words, but you and your friends ostracised them, and never let them into your little clique, did you. Just think how much happier their childhoods would have been, had you'd just been pleasant to them once in a while."

"Nice to them!" Jan retorted, "Hark whose talking? As I remember it, you were forever getting into fights and beating people up!" Jan had developed - what I can only call - a triumphant tone to her voice when she made that statement.

"Sorry to disappoint you girl, but I never smacked any bugger around who didn't deserve a good hiding in the first place, or picked a fight with me. I can look at the world in the eye with a completely clear conscience."

"What do you mean, that they deserved a good hiding?"

"The bullies in that school, girl. The shits who knocked the little kids about and stole their dinner money and the like."

"Oh, a real Robin Hood were you? Looking after the smaller children." She replied sarcastically. "I suppose I'm expected to believe that butter wouldn't melt in your mouth.

"Yeah, that just about sums it up!" I replied with a chuckle.

"Don't talk rubbish! I can remember you beating-up Jane Hunter's brother."

"Damned bloody right I did! Broke the little shits nose and knocked a few teeth out in the process." I grinned back at her, as I began fitting the spare wheel onto the hub. I've got to admit, I was enjoying the exchange.

"Well Clive Hunter was a nice boy and that was way after we all left school anyway; so he couldn't have been stealing the smaller children's' dinner money at that age. You just beat him up for the fun of it."

"What would YOU know of Clive Hunter?" I asked

"Not much, but Jane was a friend of mine, so I know he's a nice person." She replied.

"You think?" Then it was my turn to sound sarcastic. "Well, tell me something. Everyone in town knew that I gave the little shit a spanking. But what good reason can you come up with for me never being prosecuted for duffing the little shit up? Christ, it was right outside the cinema and there must have been a couple of dozen witnesses at least."

"How the hell would I know?" She retorted.

I grinned at her. "Well, I'd suggest that you find out then, Jan. Especially, before you go shouting around about how nice a bloke, Clive Hunter is or was. That's if you can find him! I'm willing to bet he's out of the country by now, what with these DNA tests they're doing nowadays. Quite a few of the old cases are suddenly turning up back in court again."

"I haven't got the faintest idea what you are talking about." Jan said, with a kind of "I give up!" tone to her voice.

"Let's put it this way Jan: Clive Hunter, with the help of your darling friend Jane and their parents, thought he'd got clean away with it. I just handed out a bit of rough justice and I'd do it again, should the occasion require. Of course, at the time, I didn't know they were going to develop these DNA tests, and I doubt Jane and her parents did either. I wonder whether they'll be done for perverting the course of justice now. They lied to the police, you know; I think you can serve time for doing that nowadays. It'd be funny seeing the much respected Councillor Hunter doing a stretch in Pentonville."

"I think you've gone soft in the head, probably from all that fighting. May I get back into my car now?"

"Yeah, go for it, girl; the wheels on, so nothing drastic is going to happen."

I finished winding the jack down and put it and the punctured wheel in the back of the car.

"All done, drop the wheel in at the garage and Pete will sort it for you," I told her. "See you around Proud Mary"

Jan gave me one more dismissive look, slapped the Disco into reverse so that she could back away from Bonnie, then took off out of the lay-by at speed heading back the way she had come.

"Thanks!" I said to myself on her behalf. Then I got back on the bike and made off towards the Green King pub, for a pint and some lunch. Thinking back to those school days when I'd taken great delight in winding up Janet Symonds and her group of friends. By loudly commenting heads up lads here comes the Proud Mary's. The nickname I gave to Janet and stuck up mates back in our schooldays.

"Jesus Tug, what did you say to that woman the other day?" Pete asked, when I called into the garage again, a couple of days later. "She was well upset with you when she turned up here."

"I didn't have to say much, Pete. We went to the same school in back in London and, well, she was a right stuck-up little bitch at the best of times. I just reminded her of who I was."

"Well, she wasn't too happy when she turned up here. Looked to me like she'd been crying."

"Ah, don't blame that one on me, Pete; she looked like she'd thrown a wobbly before I even got there. I think she had to pull herself together, to have a go at me." I grinned back at him. "Probably threw a tantrum because she'd had the puncture, that's the kind of woman she is."

"Well, she's always been very nice around here, until the other day that is. She nigh-on tore me a new arsehole for sending you out there, I can tell you.

Anyway, the strange thing is, she came in again this morning, all apologies and left this for you." Pete waved a twenty note in my direction.

"Give it back to her Pete, I don't charge women for getting them out of a tight spot, you know that; even old bats like Mrs Janet Halfon."

"That's what I told her you'd say. I'll give it back to her the next time she comes in."

Well, I thought that was going to be the end of the matter. I never expected Pete to mention Mrs Janet Halfon to me again and I had no intention mentioning her to anyone. But about three weeks later.

"Here Tug, you remember the bird with the flat tyre?" Pete asked as I was sat on one of the benches in his workshop drinking coffee with the boys.

"Yeah, why, what have I done to upset her now?" I grinned back at him.

"Well, she came in when I wasn't here the other day and was asking the boys all about you."

"Just being nosy I suspect. Did she ask them where I lived?"

"Yeah, she did." Steve, Pete's chief mechanic joined in the conversation. "But we didn't tell her. I told her, you enjoy your privacy. We just thought you'd like to know that she was asking about you; that's one tasty little number."

"Tasty she might be Steve, but I remember the bitch from my school days. A right little cow, I can assure you! We all called her Proud Mary to wind her up"

"Folks can change you know, Tug." Steve replied, "Maybe she's got the hots for you, Tug."

"Somehow I doubt that Steve. From my knowledge of the bitch, I suspect that she's after suing me for something. Besides, even if she needed a real man, I don't play with the married ones; you know that."

"Pull the other one!" Steve retorted, with a grin on his face.

I believe that Pete thought Steve might be trespassing onto the delicate ground by then; he butted in and changed the subject.

It must have been about another month or so after that. I'd been away upcountry for a few days, visiting my sister and her husband.

Jean did all my proofreading and editing for me, kind of kept it in the family sort of thing, and she and her husband Don could always use the money. Since my sister's first husband ran-off with her share of our father's ill-gotten gains, I'd done my best to help Jean financially, as much as I could. However, my philanthropy only goes so far; my sister's second husband Don has to work for his living.

To be honest, the master plan had always been, that should anyone ever come near to working it all out, Jean was going to pretend that she was the author instead of me. Yeah, you'll probably understand why later, but let's not go into all that, just yet.

Where was I? Oh yeah, I'd just come back home after spending a few days at Jean and Don's.

Well, I'd stopped off at the Sainsbury's to buy some essentials: you know eggs, milk and the like. It was still quite early because I'd left Jean's at first light and I hadn't had any breakfast that morning, so as the place wasn't too crowded I thought I'd grab a bite in the shop's cafeteria.

There I was, tucking into my eggs and somewhat questionable-looking bacon, when a voice asked, "May I join you, please, Tug?"

I looked up and there stood Mrs Janet Halfon "It's a free country, you can sit where you like, your ladyship. But there are plenty of other empty tables." I replied, I would rather the bitch sat elsewhere else; but I'm not usually rude to folks, even if I can't stand the sight of them. It was just that the morning I changed Jan's wheel, I'd had a bad night.

I didn't want anyone's company while I ate, Jan's even less than most. All the leather gear that I usually wore was designed to keep most folks of my age, at arm's length.

"Yes, I know there are other seats available, but I need to apologise to you, Tug," Jan said, taking the chair opposite me and placing her cup of coffee on the table in front of her.

"What for?" I asked.

"I'm sorry, but I had some rather unpleasant news the morning that I had that puncture. I was upset and I think I took it out on you."

"Nothing unusual!" I mumbled under my breath. Jan either never heard my remark or chose to ignore it, because she went on.

"It was very kind of you to come out and change that wheel for me. I had no idea that you did not work for the garage and were just doing Pete and myself, a favour."

"You're welcome," I replied curtly. "I'd do the same for anyone."

"So I gather now, and that makes me feel very embarrassed, considering how I went off at you..."

"Look, Jan, I wasn't feeling too bright myself that day, and I know I wound you up a bit, on purpose. I really should be apologising to you..."

"No no, Tug you were speaking the truth. I was a complete bitch at school and so were most of my friends. We ... I was never too kind to Ann or Sue and most of the other girls if it comes down to it. I was an unbelievably arrogant teenager! I don't know how I came to be that way."

I think I was supposed to say something at this point, but I chose not to. The only reply I could have given her was, "Because you were one beautiful young woman and you bloody-well knew it! And your daddy had plenty of dough, so you had it figured that the world should swoon at your feet: you stuck-up bitch!" But for some reason one of my father's old sayings came to mind, "If you can't think of anything nice to say, then say nothing!" Well, my dad was a little more colloquial in his choice of words. Didn't mince his words and never stood on ceremony, did my father.

"After the day I had that puncture," Jan continued, "I did some thinking and I asked a few friends about the Hunters. You were quite right about Clive Hunter and his family as well. How did they manage to keep it all so quiet?" she asked.

"Simple, Jan. Hunter's old man was something big on the council and he was on the police committee as well. So when the girl pointed her finger at Clive boy, daddy had the clout to keep her allegations hushed up. What with mummy, daddy and blue-eyed girl Jane all supplying him with a nice alibi, there was no chance of Clive Hunter ever being charged with anything.

"That's why they daren't have me arrested or charged with duffing the little shit up. I planned to stand in the witness box and tell the world exactly why I broke his bleeding nose, and they knew it. I've gathered since that wasn't the first nor last time that Clive Hunter has been accused of abusing a woman. I think he's out of the country now though."

"Yes, that's what I heard. A friend of mine, whose husband works for the Met police in London, said they'd asked the Hunter family to provide DNA samples for comparison, but the Hunters refused. The only reason that I could come up with of for them doing that, is that Clive Hunter did attack that girl and they know it."

"Don't worry, I know he did. He was heard bragging about scoring that night and I saw the girl a couple of days later, two black eyes and a split lip. Yeah, he scored all right; the bugger raped her. But unfortunately, she had a little bit of a reputation, so next to the Hunter family, she was classed as an unreliable witness. Consequently, the police dropped it before the little shit was even charged. I figured that I'd explain exactly why I gave the little prat a pasting from the witness box; the papers would have to report it then." I explained.

"And I suppose, what you said about those fights that you had in school was true as well. You were playing Robin Hood."

"Yeah well, some of the time. Look, Jan, boys will be boys and fight each other; that's all part of growing up. So most of the fights I got into were just us boys sorting out the pecking order. But I sorted out a few of the bullies at school while I was at it. I think that's why I was never expelled or anything; the teachers knew who the bullies were, don't you worry."

"Well Tug, I apologise for being such a bitch when we were children and for being so bitchy with you the other day. God, I should have been grateful you were changing my wheel. I'm sorry, I'd had a bad day."

"Don't let it worry you Jan, and I told you I wasn't in the best of moods myself. I could have defused the situation if I'd thought about it. How long had you been sat there waiting anyway."

"Only about an hour. Oh god, Tug, that wasn't what I was upset about, I'd had some bad news that morning, and it had shaken me up quite a bit. You were the first person I ran into that I could take it out on. Talk about the kettle calling the pot black! I was on my way to scratch some bitch's eyes out if I could have got up the nerve when I got that puncture."

Quite suddenly, Jan burst into tears. To be honest I had no idea what to make of it. I had no clue what are you supposed to do in those kinds of circumstances, I looked around and noted that Jan and I had become the centre of attention in the sparsely populated cafeteria. I glared at anyone who caught my eye and pretty soon they were all trying to pretend that they hadn't noticed that Jan was crying.

"I'm sorry, things get on top of me and I get emotional all the time lately. My marriage is going wrong, Tug, and I don't know what to do about it." Jan said, finally getting her emotions back under some control after about five minutes sobbing.

I had handed her my clean handkerchief and she mopped her eyes with it - annihilating her make-up, once again. I got the feeling that was becoming a habit for the woman.

"I've had the same problem myself, Jan. It'll pass, I can assure you. It just takes a little time. Believe me, I know."

Jan looked into my eyes and I was surprised to see a concerned expression come over her face. Although she had no idea why my marriage had gone down the pan, I'm sure the woman felt sympathy for me, even with her troubles: whatever they were.

"I do think that you need to undertake some running repairs, Jan," I suggested, with a gentle smile on my face.

Jan pulled a little hand mirror out of her bag. "Oh god!" she exclaimed. "Don't go away Tug, I'll be back in a minute," she said as she jumped out of her seat and headed off towards the ladies toilets.

I pushed the rest of my breakfast around the plate; what was left wasn't very appetising and was pretty well cold. I think I was debating leaving before Jan returned. I didn't need to hear about her troubles and was suspecting that I soon would.

Come on, I didn't like the woman; I was just being polite by talking to her.

And there was another thing, that looks of concern that came on her face when I'd hinted that my marriage had gone down the tubes. I was pretty sure that she intended enquiring about that, and Laura was one subject that I preferred to avoid.

Quite suddenly Jan was back.

"I'm sorry, I get emotional so easily nowadays, Tug. You see, I'm not the ice maiden you seem to believe that I am." She smiled at me. "Now tell me what happened between you and ... Laura, it was Laura Jones you married wasn't it?"

Yeah, and how did I know that Jan was going to ask that? Mind you I was wondering how Jan had known that I had married Laura, as I'd lost track of most of our school peers by the time Laura Jones and I had got together.

Laura Jones you mean," I replied. "She insisted that we got married whilst I was in the Marines. I should have known better really."

"You joined the Royal Marines?" Anne repeated, with a questioning tone to her voice. I figured, like most folks, Jan hadn't envisaged that I'd ever join up instead of working for my Dad. I ignored her statement and continued.

"Things went all right for a few years. Well, things were pretty tight financially and I think Laura suddenly realised that there were guys out there who earned a lot more dosh that I did. Eventually, she buggered-off whilst I was playing silly buggers down in the Falklands she shacked up with one of the big cheeses at the place she was working."

"Oh, dear!" Jan said, with that concerned expression returning to her face again. "What a bitch; I always thought Laura was such a nice person."

Generally, I didn't like to discuss what had happened between Laura and myself with anyone. So I have no explanation as to why I sat there and told Jan all about it. Let's face it, the cafeteria of a Sainsbury's early on a Saturday morning isn't the place to have such a discussion with anyone, anyway.

"Well to be honest maybe she was." I found myself saying. "Possibly Laura was beguiled by the money and lifestyle that the wanker offered her. But it didn't last long. After the divorce was final and Laura mentioned the magic word to him, he soon found a replacement and kicked her out."

"Magic word?" Jan asked.

"Yeah, marriage! From what I've gathered through the grapevine, once the decree absolute was issued Laura started talking about wedding bells, and super-stud told her that he already had her replacement lined up. You know she dared to come crying on my doorstep and asked me to take her back."

"Oh my god, she didn't!" Jan exclaimed. "Did you ever think about it? Taking her back, I mean."

"Not on your bloody life, Jan; I'd loved the woman more than I can say. But how could I ever trust her again? What would happen the next time some handsome git with a big chequebook turned up? It broke my heart to turn her away, but I didn't have much choice. I was hoping to have some children some time and I've no intention of bringing up kids in a broken home." I explained.

"That's my problem at the moment, and I don't know what I'm going to do," Jan said, the tears reappearing in her eyes again. "My husband's moved his dolly bird from the office into a flat in London. He lives with her during the week and comes home to stay with us on the weekends, basically to take the children out. He seems to think that I should accept the fact that he's got a mistress, put up with it and carry on as if nothing has changed."

"Do bleeding what?" It was my turn to react in shock then. "And what are you intending to do about it?"

Look I'd wouldn't like anyone to get the idea that I liked Jan. To be perfectly honest I didn't know her as an individual, and she was a type of person that I didn't like to associate with. However, having been ... shat upon from a great height, myself, I didn't like the idea that Jan's husband was doing the same thing to her. Kind-a annoyed me somewhat!

"I don't know that there is anything much that I can do, Tug," Jan replied. "I've kicked him out of our bedroom of course, but that doesn't seem to have worried him in the least. He just says..." Jan stopped speaking, I believe she was wondering about how much she should tell me. Then her facial expression changed. I could see that she'd decided on some kind.

"Tug, I haven't told anyone about this. I haven't got anyone that I feel I can trust nowadays, well not around here anyway. But for some reason, I believe I can talk to you, in confidence. Would you mind?" she asked.

That was an interesting question, "Would I mind?" Damn it, I think my soft heart came to the fore again. The damned thing had always been my Achilles heel.

"No Jan, I don't mind at all, and I can promise you that I do know how to keep my mouth shut. But I don't think this is the place for a heart to heart chat about anything. I think we should go somewhere with a little more privacy, but public enough for decency."

"Oh yes, that's the best idea," Jan said looking around the cafeteria. The place was beginning to fill up a bit by then.

"How about I'll meet you at Pete's Garage in twenty minutes?" I suggested. "We can use his office, it's public enough with those big glass windows, but it's also pretty soundproof. And we both could have legitimate reasons for being there. What's so unusual about a couple of old school friends having a chat whilst they wait for their cars to be fixed?"

"Why are you being so nice to me, Tug?" Jan asked.

"I don't know, Jan. I think it's a basic and very fatal flaw in my personality; I'm a mug for a sob story. I try to play the evil bastard, but I can't keep the front up, all of the time."

She smiled at me as we left the table.

Damn, I thought to myself, if only the bitch had given me that smile now and again when we were back at school. Jan sure was a good looking woman. I couldn't for the life of me figure out what her husband was playing at.

Half an hour later we were ensconced in Pete's office. Jan's Land Rover Discovery was up on one of the ramps, with the young lad wandering around beneath it, grease gun in hand, trying to look like he was doing something. Pete served up a couple of mugs of coffee and then withdrew, giving me a sly wink as he closed the door.

"Tell me more about what happened between you and Laura please, Tug; did she believe that you'd take her back?" Jan asked.

I figured Jan had turned shy again and wanted me to kind of re-break the ice.

"Yes, she came knocking on my door about two o'clock one morning, threw herself into my arms and begged me to forgive her."

"But you wouldn't?"

"It wasn't so much that I wouldn't, Jan: more that I couldn't. Oh, believe me, I wanted to, I'd been crazy about that woman for years, by then. But once someone's done something like Laura did to me, you just can't take the chance! God, I almost topped myself when she walked out on me in the first place. There was no way I could risk putting myself through that again."

"Is that why you steer clear of women now?" She asked.

"What gave you that idea?"

"Tug, I'm sorry, I've been asking around about you. I was quite surprised! There are not very many folks in this town who know you personally. And strangely, for a handsome guy like yourself, no one admits to ever seeing you with a girlfriend or anything. As a matter of fact, for such a high profile bloke, riding about on that motorcycle of yours all the time, no one seems to know very much about you at all. And those that do, like Pete and the boys here, keep their mouths firmly closed."

"So, what's that supposed to prove?"

"Well let's just say that the girl's at the gym and the hairdresser's, have all noticed you. I find it funny that I had never spotted you myself until you fixed my tyre the other day. And even then I didn't realise that you were the guy that I'd heard the girls mention so many times. Quite a few of them have cast their eyes in your direction. You know, none of them knew whether you are married or not, they all just assumed that you were a bachelor."

"Probably thought I was a bloody poofter," I suggested.

"Oh no, quite definitely not, Tug. Raymondo, the guy who owns the hairdressers is a homosexual you know, and he's assured the girls that you're not into that scene."

"Nice of him!" I added sarcastically.

"Oh, he's quite a nice man once you get to know him, Tug. He's possibly the only other person that I could have talked to about Andrew. But I didn't think that was a good idea, the hairdressers are always rife with rumour and gossip, and Raymondo might just let something slip."

"Yeah that's a point, we are here to talk about you and your problems, not mine Jan."

"Yes I know, but it's embarrassing for me to talk about."

"Well don't be embarrassed with me, Jan. I told you, I've been there and as you so rightly point out, no one in town knows me, so I won't go spreading gossip."

Jan gave me another strange look. "Yes, I've got to talk this out with someone who hasn't got an axe to grind. My mother says I should grin and bear it. She says that some men are like that, it's a phase they go through when they think they are getting old."

"Jesus, how old is Andrew?" I asked.

"Same age as us, thirty-six."

"Bit young for a mid-life crisis, don't you think? More like he's forgotten where his priorities lie if you ask me. So tell me, what happened at home?"

Jan started to cry again.

"Come on Jan, crying ain't gonna solve anything."

"Yes I know, but I'm so hurt that he could do such a thing to me ... and the children." She said struggling to get her emotions back under control.

Personally, I was beginning to think that Randy Andy bleeding Halfon needed a kick up the jacksy. What's more, I feared that I'd probably be the one that had to give it to him, one day. I'd just have to work it so that he took the first swing; I doubted I'd find that too difficult to arrange. It was an art, I'd developed during my teenage years.

"About a year or so ago," Jan began, "Andrew got very busy at the office, or so he claimed; I'm not so sure I believe that now though. Anyway, he said that he had to stay over at a hotel in London some nights because he claimed he'd finished work far too late to drive home. As time went on the nights in London got more and more frequent and then eventually he announced that he was buying a flat up in town because it would be cheaper than the hotel bills."

Jan had been looking at the floor, now she looked up at me.

"The nights he spent away became more and more frequent. In the end, he was just coming home on the weekends. Friday night to start with, but later he took to turning up on Saturday mornings and leaving again late Sunday afternoon."

"Sounds about par for the course," I interjected.

"You know, I must be thick or something, I didn't see what was going on right in front of my eyes. But he was my husband, I trusted him!"

"Yeah, dodgy thing trust, I've made the same mistake myself," I interjected again.

"Well, then one day someone called the house and told me that Andrew had some little tart living in that flat with him. I called them a liar because I couldn't believe my husband would do that to me. But a couple of nights later I called the flat when I knew that Andrew was in

Berlin for a meeting and ... well, she answered the damn telephone. You see, she wasn't expecting me to call, as I'd always called Andrew on his mobile telephone in the past: he had been very insistent that I do that."

"So what did you do, challenge him when he got home?"

"I should have done, but I went off half-cocked and left an angry message on his voice mail. By the time Andrew did get home, he'd had plenty of time to prepare for my attack. To put it bluntly, he called my bluff. Andrew told me he was going to have some fun whilst he was still young enough and he didn't care whether he stayed married to me or not. He told me that if I didn't like him having a mistress, then I should divorce him."

"What, just like that? Like it or lump it. Why the hell didn't you just kick him out?"

"Well I think I wanted to, but as I said, he was all prepared and he'd done his homework. Andrew had seen a rather clever solicitor who specialises in divorce.

He had it all worked out, how much child support he'd have to pay and even how much alimony I'd get. And it wasn't very much after what I've been used to living on, I can assure you. Andrew's an accountant by profession and he's pretty slick at hiding his true worth from the authorities; he's been doing that for years."

"You know I haven't got the faintest idea when he moved all of his private files out of the house, that's where all the details of his off-shore money were kept. So he must have realised that I would find out about his little tart sometime and he was all prepared for me."

"You haven't said that he asked you for a divorce, Jan?"

"Well no, he claims that he doesn't want one. He's quite happy with the status quo, he wants his tart during the week and to come home to his children at the weekends. I think he believes I'll let him back into my bedroom eventually."

"You are, kidding me!"

"No Andrew seems to believe that when I've gone without for long enough, I'll beg him to ... You know, sleep with me again."

"Ooh-er, got some bloody front, hasn't he! Why don't you just kick the bugger out and find yourself another man? You're a good looking woman Jan, you must have had plenty of guys hit on you all the time."

Jan fixed me with her eyes. "Well for a start, because I love the bastard, and I want my marriage back how it use to be. I thought I'd try to grin and bear it, but it gets harder all the time. Besides as Andrew says, what man wants a wife with a ready-made family?"

"So he's led you to believe that the children are going to make a difference to any man who's attracted to you?" I asked.

"Well, he said that the men who have made passes at me in the last few years have only done so because they figure that I'm safe because I'm married and they won't expect anything other than a quick roll in the hay.

Andrew says that if we get divorced I'll get plenty of men who'll be happy to take me to bed, but they won't be wanting a fulltime relationship because of the children."

"You don't believe all that crap, do you? Its bloody nonsense. The end of a marriage doesn't mean the end of the world, you know. I know lots of people who are very happy in their second marriage after the first one went tits-up on them."

"Yes, I have a few friends who are on their second marriage. But only one of them has children from their first relationship, and they haven't been the easiest children to handle. If it wasn't for her husband being very patient, I think they would have been divorced again by now."

"Well that proves the lie to Andrew's theory about guys only wanting a roll in the hay then doesn't it? Sounds to me like your friend's found someone who's fairly well committed to making his relationship with her work. You see, they are out there; you just have to find one of them. Jan, I don't think it's worth hanging onto a marriage where your husband doesn't respect you."

"But I love him!" She said with an exasperated tone to her voice.

"Jan, can you love a man whose treated you like Andrew has for the last year? Or is it that you've got used to the nice cosy life you had, and you're scared of what the future might hold? If you think that Andrew really does still love you and he'll eventually get tired of his little tart, kick him out and go see a solicitor about a divorce. If he does love you, he'll start eating humble pie quick enough and come back into line when he discovers you won't stand for his fun and games anymore."

"And if he doesn't and lets the divorce go through, I'll have lost everything."

"No, you'll still have your children and your pride. And strangely enough, if he wants to stay in contact with his children, you'll be pulling the strings."

"Oh, I couldn't do that to Andrew. He loves the children."

"You also said that Andrew loved you. It sounds to me that your husband has a very high opinion of himself. I'm sorry, but I suspect that even if he did love you once, he doesn't love you anymore; he just likes to control you."

Jan suddenly got angry with me then. "This was a mistake, I should have known better than to talk to you about this!"

She stood up and headed for the door. Before I could stop her, Jan was in her car and driving away.

"What was all that about?" Pete asked as I came out of his office.

"Don't ask, Pete. This never happened, neither of us were here this morning, okay."

"Whatever you say Tug. She is a looker though."

"Pete, she was a bitch when we were at school. Now, she's a mixed-up bitch with a very big problem."

You don't like her then?"

"No Pete, I don't think I do. She says she's changed, but I think she's still the bitch she always was and that could be the cause of her problems. Look, I've said too much just keep your nose out of it."

"Jean, do you remember Janet Symonds?" I asked. It was a couple of weeks later and I'd popped back up to Jean's place to go over my latest revisions.

"Yeah, of course, I do. You used to wind her up calling her Proud Mary and singing that song. Why what suddenly brings her to mind?"

"Ah, she's married and lives not too far from me. I ran into her the other week and..." I stopped speaking, I wasn't sure what I was going to say to my sister about Jan, or why I'd brought the subject up.

"And what? Don't tell me you fancy her - you hated the girl's guts at school. Besides, you know better than to mess with married women." Jean said quite sternly.

"No, she's got a problem. Her old man's running around on her. Found himself a mistress!" I went on to outline everything that Jan had told me at the garage.

"Sounds familiar." Jean retorted. "If the woman's got any sense, she should get shot of the bugger a bit sharpish. It was the best move that I ever made."

"That's what I told her, but I think the silly cow wants to win him back," I replied.

"Silly bitch! Mind she always was pretty sure of herself."

"Well, I don't think she is now. Her old man seems to have convinced her that she'd have trouble replacing him. I think he's got her pretty well brainwashed that she's lost her looks and her ability to attract the right sort of man. He's got her convinced that if she loses him she'll turn out either an old maid or every Tom, Dick and Harry's toy."

"Sounds to me that she didn't attract the right sort of man in the first place. What do you intend to do about it, Tug?" Jean asked.

"Me? Nothing, it's none of my business."

"Come on, I know my brother! What would one of your heroine's do in the circumstances?"

"I don't know, divorce the bugger and then some White Knight would come riding over the horizon and sweep her off her feet. But she doesn't want a divorce, she wants her husband back." I replied.

"Then she's a fool then, Tug. I tell you what though; I should imagine that he's so arrogant that he does think that she won't find anyone to replace him. Maybe he needs to realise that he'd not the only fish in the pond." Jean said with a grin on her face.

"Oh, and how do we achieve that?" I asked.

"We can't brother, but you can. You've got all the right attributes: you're single, rich and handsome."

"Don't flatter me, Sis."

"It's true Tug, and think about it; he doesn't know you does he?"

"Doubt it. I don't expect we move in the same circles. He works in the City I think."

"Then he definitely won't know you, unless you've threatened to punch the bugger on the nose at some time. Anyway, if you were to show some interest in Jan, it might make the silly-arse sit up and take notice. That's if bugger even realises that you are sniffing around."

"Jean, I don't even like the woman!"

"I know that, but you're not going to marry her, Tug. All you're going to do is show the man that if he doesn't pull his socks-up and start behaving himself. Then someone else could come along and steal Jan from under his nose."

"I'm not sure I like the sound of this, Jean. Suppose it gets out of hand."

"Just think of the novel you can base on it, Tug. You'll be laughing all the way to the bank on this one."

Okay, I have no idea why I even contemplated Jean's idea, or why I'd involved myself in Jan's marital problems in the first place. But on my way back home the following morning, I began to formulate a plan. I'd start very gently and see what happened.

The first move was pretty obvious, for me anyway. I needed some information about Jan, her husband, and his tart and their movements.

I did a little research in town (London) that first weekend and then I needed to case out Jan's home to get the general layout of the area.

Jan's house was on an estate of fairly new houses, maybe ten or twenty years old. It wasn't all that far from my own house, in fact, maybe two miles or so, but it wasn't an area that I'd had a call to visit very often, if at all.

Like a lot of the newer estates, the houses were on small plots, unlike my Georgian pile of a house with its massive garden and coach house, that afforded me a lot of privacy. I worked out that there were a couple of places I could park and watch Jan's house without it being too obvious.

I couldn't use any of my vehicles though. The motorbike would stand out like a sore thumb, as would the Land Rover and the Rolls. Yeah, I've got myself a Rolls Royce Corniche; not new, a 1987 model, but fun to drive down to the south of France and Italy for the odd break. Look I'm a pretty well successful author even if I do hide my so-called talent under a bush. Anyway, all three of my forms of transport tended to get noticed.

My stakeout car of choice was Steve's (from the garages) BMW or Pete's cherished Audi Quatro, both of which had tinted side windows. They were happy to loan their vehicles to me. I'd chauffeured both of them to and from their weddings in the Rolls.

I'd figured that the only person I had to worry about spotting me was Jan, but I forgot about nosy neighbours. On the fourth day of my stakeout, the local beat copper's car pulled up behind me.

Luckily I was acquainted with the officer because my home was also on his patch; I'd met him once before when someone tried to break into the coach house. I had my laptop on my lap and was banging away at the keys when he knocked on the window. I gave him some fool yarn about having the decorators in and needing somewhere quiet to work. I'm not sure he bought the story completely, but he went off satisfied. I was to see him drive past me a few times during the following couple of weeks.

Anyway from my stakeout position, I learnt Jan's routine. Which basically -- besides running the Children to school, doing some shopping, two visits to the gym and one to the beauty parlour come hairdressers a week -- amounted to messing around in her garden. And, I assume, doing her housework. I never noticed anyone who looked like a cleaner visit the house. I never saw anyone visit the place.

The weekends I had difficulty getting my head around for a while. Andrew would arrive home in his Jag at around nine-thirty on Saturday morning. Five minutes later Jan would leave the house and head for the Sainsbury's Supermarket where I'd run into her that morning. She'd wander around the place for hours often going to the cafeteria several times for coffee etc. Then she'd leave the place and head into town, where she'd meander around the shops for a while before taking in an afternoon matinee at the cinema.

Jan would arrive home again just after six. Shortly after she'd arrived Andrew would leave the house with the two children. God knows where he took them; I never followed him. But all the lights in the house, except the one over the front door, would go out about nine o'clock-ish. I figured Jan went to bed before Andrew returned with the children at just after eleven.

I missed Jan on the first Sunday morning because she was out of the house early. I only realised that she'd already gone because her car was missing from the drive. I discovered later that she was leaving home at six AM on Sunday mornings and heading for the gym.

Luckily I spotted her Disco in the sports centre car park. She spent several hours in there, before going to a golf driving range and venting her spleen on more than one bucket of balls.

Shit, that woman could drive a golf ball some way, when she was upset. I was able to get close enough to see the anger in her face, mainly because she was so lost in smashing those balls as hard as she possibly could, that she failed to notice me standing there watching her.

Jan had Sunday lunch alone, in a small restaurant in town; then sat in the park until around four-thirty, when she drove home again. Andrew left the house shortly after Jan had arrived there.

I came to the obvious conclusion that Jan was trying to stay out of the house whilst Andrew was at home. But I had no idea if she was doing so of her own volition, or because Andrew had requested she did. Whatever, after some thought on the subject I decided that a shove of some kind was required to bring things to ahead. Although I still wasn't convinced that I was doing the right thing by getting involved, I was curious about what would happen.

The catalyst I chose was a simple bouquet. Not any flowers, Red roses and a dozen of the buggers, to boot. I added a nice little note

'Janet Symonds, Though you belong to another, I love you anyway!' you're still Proud Mary to me'.

Then had them delivered at exactly six PM on the following Saturday afternoon, just before Jan usually arrived home.

I was parked in my spot just a few hundred yards from Jan's house when the florist's delivery van arrived. I watched the guy get the bouquet from the back of the van and approach the front door, which opened before he got to it. The two children came out first; I suspect that they had been watching for their mother to return and saw the guy heading for that house with the flowers.

Jan's husband came out, shooed the children back inside and closed the door. Then he had a brief conversation with the florist's driver before I saw Andrew take the card from the bouquet and look at it. I'm not sure exactly what he made of that card, but it certainly took him by surprise; that was clear to see from his body language. I could see that he was asking the delivery driver something, but the young man just kept shrugging his shoulders and holding out the flowers for Andrew to take. The thing was, at the same time Andrew kept reading the card over and over again.

Then Andrew suddenly put the card back in its little envelope and shoved that back in amongst the flowers of the bouquet again. The florist's driver repositioned it carefully, whilst Andrew started waving his arms about. I couldn't hear what was being said, but Andrew's body language led me to believe that he was telling the driver to "Take the bloody flowers away with him!", or something along those lines anyway.

Unfortunately for Andrew, the driver wasn't going to play ball on that one. The young man was aware that I was watching, and he also knew that a tenner tip depended on him delivering the flowers at exactly the right time and that if Andrew refused to accept them, the driver should still be hanging around trying to deliver the bloody things when Jan arrived home. Which she did, precisely on schedule at ten past six!

I watched as the guy spoke to Jan and then handed her the bouquet. Andrew had turned around and stomped back into the house, his body language once again demonstrating that he wasn't happy about something. Through my binoculars, I saw Jan watch him go and I'm pretty well sure that - just for an instant - I could make out a smirk on her face. Then she took some money from her purse and tipped the driver, before following Andrew inside.

The van driver stopped beside the BMW and came around to collect his tenner, with a big smile on his face.

"You've got one upset husband there, mate. I have to assume that was your intention!" He grinned, as I gave him his money.

I just smiled back at him and put my finger to my lips.

"Sure thing mister, whatever you say." He replied then he drove away in his van.

Andrew and the children left the house later than they had the previous two Saturdays. Even at that range, I could sense that there was an atmosphere; body language again. The odd thing was both the children were grinning like Cheshire cats. And as Andrew's car drew level with the BMW which Jan's son appeared to take great interest in it. Although he couldn't see me inside because of the tinted side windows, I'd swear blind the little bugger grinned and even winked at me.

About seven-thirty, Jan came out of the house dressed up to the nines. She reversed her car out of the drive and then took off in the opposite direction to the one I was parked in. I let her get to the corner before I began to follow her. Jan then drove on a very convoluted route to the sports centre -- not somewhere I thought she get dressed up like she was for -- and went inside.

I tucked the BMW in a dark corner of the car park and settled down to wait until Jan came out again. The place was fairly quiet at that time on a Saturday evening; I'd risk being spotted by Jan if I went inside.

It was only about ten minutes later when — taking me completely by surprise - the car's nearside door suddenly swung open and Jan sat in the passenger seat.

"I should report you for stalking me, you bastard! What the hell do you think you are playing at, sending me those damned flowers?" she demanded, but confusingly, with a grin on her face.

In a state of shock by Jan's sudden appearance, I couldn't think what to say to her for a minute or two. Not that she gave me time to say much anyway.

"When that man handed me those roses, I was completely flummoxed for a little while. And then I started to put two and two together. I'm not sure what brought it to mind, but when I read that card ... It was what you used to call me and that song you used to sing in the school concerts, wasn't it? Only I couldn't remember the damned words of that song at first. Except the song was by Creedence Clearwater Your party piece."

"Yeah well, can I help it if I sound like John Fogerty when I sing that one. I wondered whether you'd pick-up on the clue." I replied.

"It took me a few minutes, but when my son James mentioned that he saw the florist's van had stopped by the black BMW. James is mad about cars and he'd noticed it earlier in the week; he also said that he thought it was the same one that is sometimes parked at the garage. I suddenly realised that it was probably you and guessed what you were playing at. You're trying to make Andrew jealous, aren't you?"

"Well, that was a general idea, Jan. And to make him realise that he's not the only fish in the sea." I explained.

"Yes well, with the way we've got on in the past, I did realise that the sentiment in the flowers and card, was all for Andrew's benefit. You haven't got any silly ideas in your head about you and me, have you?"

"Come on, Jan. Me, with a stuck-up up Proud Mary little bitch like Janet Symonds? Kind of like chalk and cheese, don't you think?" I replied.

"Well, that's a relief," she said smiling again. "But I suspected that you're back to playing your Robin Hood character again. Anyway, you know what? I think it might have worked. Andrew was beside himself and was demanding to know who had sent them. I didn't know what to say to him at first. But then I thought, "So what?" and told him that if he could play around, then, what was to stop me doing the same thing? I don't think he liked that!"

"Well good on you girl, it's about time you stood up for yourself."

"I just hope it doesn't backfire and he walks out on me and the children for good."

"So, what if he does, tell me what would you have lost? A guy who has no respect for you and who's been taking the piss out of you for god knows how long."

"He's my husband, Tug. I took some vows remember, 'Until death do us part'."

"And I assume, he took a vow that included 'Forsaking all others!', Jan!"

"Yeah, you got a point there. But I've got to try to win him back." She said again.

"Not that I can see he's worth chasing. You'll never be able to trust the bugger again, whatever happens, you do realise that!" I warned her.

"That's my problem Tug, not yours!" Jan said and then she went quiet for a few seconds. "Right, okay then, where are you taking me tonight. I have to be out of the house with my bit on the side when Andrew and the children get home. So you're lumbered with either trailing me around all night like I suspect you have been doing all week or taking me somewhere ... nice."

"Well Jan, if you want to play the game, then we'd better find an out of the way pub, somewhere where no one will know us, or you at least."

I started the car and headed out of town to the Ponderosa, a little village pub that I regularly use. The governor is a country music fan, which he had playing quietly in the background all the time.

I've got to say we got some strange looks when I arrived. I'd never been there with a female companion before, let alone one who scrubbed-up, as well as Jan, did.

"It's nice here, they all seem to know you well enough; do you come here often? Jan asked once we settled ourselves in a quiet corner.

Before I could reply Proud Mary started coming over the sound system. I do believe a little louder than the previous tune had been playing. I gave Bert the governor "the evil look" and the bugger grinned back at me.

"Oh, sounds like they are playing your song!" Jan observed.

"Yeah, the bugger's doing it on purpose to wind me up, because you're here with me I suspect. In the summer they have a little combo who play out in the garden some evenings and everyone as to do their party piece. Mine is Proud Mary by Creedence Clearwater Revival, of course." I informed her.

"I might have guessed! Is that the only song you know?"

"No, but it's the one they always demand that I sing here. That and 'Nobody's Child'."

"I don't think I know that one," she said.

"You don't want to, Jan; not when I sing it anyway. Now, tell me something, what's with you disappearing out of the house when Andrew shows up there?" I asked.

"Humph!" Jan said, and then she stared at the table for a little while. "Andrew said he wanted to take the children out on his own when he came home to see them. They aren't best pleased with what he's been playing at."

"Did you tell them, that he's got himself a mistress, I mean?" I asked.

"You're joking! Of course, I didn't. I told them that their father was very busy at the office and didn't have the time to come home to us as much as he wanted to. Unfortunately, our children aren't dumb. They noticed the atmosphere when their father was in the house, and

I think they might have overheard us arguing about 'her'. They worked it out pretty quick and gave Andrew a lot of stick over it."

"Andrew said that it was me, turning them against him, and Tracy! I ask you, Tracy, Essex girl or what? A bloody little tart, I'll scratch her bloody eyes out if I ever run into the little cow. Anyway, Andrew insisted that he took the children out on his own. So I thought, well if that's what you want, then you can look after them completely all the time you're at the house. You know, feed them and everything.

"I went to stay with my mother and sister a couple of weekends, but I couldn't keep going there - my mother was driving me nuts saying that I should play the docile little housewife and let Andrew get it out of his system.

"I went to a health retreat a couple of times as well, but Andrew complained about the cost and put me on a tighter budget. The bugger's got me every way I turn. When I complained he just told me that I'd have to get used to not having much cash if we did divorce."

It struck me that Andrew had been playing mind games with Jan. He had her convinced that she'd be on her uppers if it did come to a divorce. The poor girl had little or no idea of how she'd live without Andrew as a provider.

"You could get a job, Jan," I suggested.

"Oh yeah, and what kind of job could I get Tug? I was only in the job market for a couple of years; Andrew walked straight into a good position at his father's firm, and he didn't want his wife working for a living. Everything's computers nowadays and I'd be completely lost."

"We've all had to find our way around computers, Jan! It's not that difficult, once you get into it. You could go to night school classes and learn how to use them."

"And who'd look after the children whilst I did? I can't afford a babysitter and even if I could, if Andrew found out what I was doing, he'd cut my budget even more."

"I'd say that sounds a little like an excuse, to me Jan. It couldn't be that you like the nice cosy life you've got used to and that's why you're willing to put up with all the Bull shit Andrew's giving you, could it?"

That was a challenge to Jan. I was still having difficulty in understanding why she hadn't thrown her husband out on his ear, the moment she'd found out about his girlfriend. Well, to be honest, our conversation got a little on the heated side after that. Jan didn't walk out on me or anything, but I got the feeling that if she'd had her car with her, she would have done.

The drive back the sports centre was conducted in stony silence, although Jan did somewhat grudgingly thank me before she got out of the car. I followed her home at a discreet distance. And after parking a little way along the road from her house, I walked back to see if I could hear a war going on. If Andrew got uppity and started, knocking Jan around, I figured I might have to do something about it. Shortly, after Jan went in at midnight the lights went out and the house was silent, so I went home.

The next morning Jan beat me again and was at the gym by the time I found her car. I figured she'd stick to her usual routine so I took the opportunity to take Steve's BMW back and collect my Land Rover that he had been using. Steve's stepchildren weren't impressed that they weren't going to be riding around in the Land Rover any more. Steve later told me they were on at him to buy one of those American Humvee's.

"Some hopes, driving the Land Rover for a couple of weeks was fun. But I think that if I went FWD I'd go for a Range Rover, the misses likes her comfort." was Steve's comment.

But the kids pointed that a Range Rover wouldn't be as much fun. I left them to their argument and made a strategic withdrawal.

I was at the driving range knocking a few balls around myself when Jan arrived. She spotted me and went into the next bay.

"That was a waste of time, Andrew's concluded that I sent those flowers to myself," she mumbled, as she tried to put her first over the boundary fence.

"Shit girl, remind me never to play a round of golf against you when you're angry; hitting the balls like that, you'd be on the green in one, every time."

"Arrogant Bastard!" She said as the next ball clanged off the side boundary as she sliced it.

"Calm down Jan. If that's what he wants to believe, then you aren't going to talk him around." I said, "We'll just up the ante and give him a real surprise next weekend, then he'll have to eat humble pie."

"How?" Jan asked.

"You'll see - he won't know what's hit him. Now empty that bucket and then I'll buy you a decent lunch and we can make war plans." I told her.

Over lunch, I asked Jan what had happened when she got home. She told me that Andrew was sitting up waiting for her and almost immediately accused her of buying the flowers herself. He made some comment about her having money to burn and hinted at reducing her allowance. Jan had stormed off to bed. But her son had come into her room and asked her if she'd had a nice evening.

"What did you tell him? No, I spent the night arguing with a boy you hated at school." I suggested.

"Well not exactly. I said I went for a quiet drink with an old school friend. Well, I did say we'd never got on when we were younger, but that you seem to have mellowed a little as you've grown older, Tug."

"Charming!" I retorted.

"Well, you have, even if you do look like a hells angel most of the time. You're not the bugger you used to be that's for sure. Although you can still be very arrogant sometimes."

"Arrogant! Hark who's talking..." I began to say.

"Tug, please let's not fight again, I have enough of fighting with Andrew." She'd asked nicely.

I didn't think I needed to follow her home that day. But I did sit in the park with Jan for a while. Hey, we fed the ducks. I hadn't done that since I'd been I nipper.

"Someone's been in here looking for you!" Pete said, with a grin on his face, when I called in the garage on Tuesday morning. "She wanted your phone number and turned quite nasty when I told her I couldn't give it to her. She says she needs to talk to you. You know, Tug, it's usual to give your girlfriends your phone number."

"Sorry Pete, I never thought about it. Anyway, she's not my girlfriend, she's just an acquaintance with a situation. I'm hoping I can help her out, that's all."

"Yeah, I believe you, but you'd better give her a..." Pete's facial expression changed as he spotted something over my shoulder. "No don't bother, here she comes. You'd better use my office again," he said, and headed for the far end of the workshop, followed by his two 'oppo's' once they'd spotted Jan's arrival as well. I went into the office to wait for her.

"This isn't going to work Tug. My daughter is accusing me of driving her father away." Jan blurted out, the moment I shut the office door.

"How does she work that one out? Andrew has virtually sodded-off with his fancy bit!" I replied.

"Yes, but that's children for you," Jan said, as she dropped herself in a chair behind Pete's desk. "Chrissie is, or was, very close to her father; she's very upset that she doesn't see him much nowadays. My daughter's under the impression that it was something that I've done that drove him away in the first place."

I had to be careful about what I said at that point. In her younger days, Jan always had been a pain in the arse, so she could well have done something to piss Andrew off. Nevertheless, what the shit was doing to her, weren't exactly cricket. I decided to keep mum and let Jan babble on.

"When I told the children that we, you and I, we're going out next Saturday night, Chrissie went ballistic. I think she, like Andrew, suspected I'd brought those flowers myself and then went out and hid somewhere for the evening the other night."

"So, what are you going to do, let your daughter control your life?" I asked. It was obvious that Andrew was, or was trying to, pull Jan's strings, and she needed to decide who was going to run her life. "Look Chrissie's going to have to face up to the situation sometime; her father is playing you for a prize mug. And to be honest

Jan, you've got to stand up for yourself or the bugger's going to walk all over you forever."

"Yes, I know you're right, Tug. But Chrissie told me last night that if her father and I separate, she wants to go live with her him!"

"Separate!" I exclaimed. "If you ask me you've separated already, Jan. All that he's using you for is a bloody housekeeper cum childminder."

"It was my idea not to sleep with Andrew anymore, Tug."

"And it was possibly the best move you've made, Jan. Christ the guy wants it all. You to look after the children and run the home, and have his little tart to play with the rest of the time."

I'm going to admit that this wanker Randy Andy Halfon was getting my goat. I was no fan of Jan's: never had been. Nevertheless, the tosser was taking the piss out the woman, more than Laura ever got near doing to me.

At least Laura had the decency to bugger-off with the shit that she took up with when she thought he loved her. Alternatively, she loved his money. I never could work out exactly what had happened there; still, that's all in the past and not worth worrying about now.

"Well if you ask me if your daughter wants to go live with her father, then you couldn't go too far wrong in encouraging her, or at least not trying to talk her out of the idea too forcefully," I suggested.

"But she's my child; I don't want to lose her." Jan retorted.

"I realise that Jan, and it hasn't come to a formal separation or divorce yet. So it's best to leave crossing that bridge until you come to the bugger. But I get the feeling that Andrew, or at least his little dolly bird Tracy, isn't going to be too enamoured with the idea of a ten-year-old girl sharing that flat with them. It's going to spike their guns a bit, for a start. I'd make a few subtle comments about boarding schools to Chrissie if I was you, and point-out that all her friends live around here."

"You don't think Andrew would put Chrissie in a boarding school, do you?"

"I don't know about what Andrew would do, Jan, but Tracy would in a bloody flash; I know the type. She's having one hell of time spending Andrew's money, I think Chrissie would suss her out, soon enough. No, Tracy would want Chrissie out of the place as fast as she could arrange it. It could drive a very nice wedge between the pair of them if you're lucky." I smiled at Jan.

"You know her, this Tracy woman?" Jan asked.

"Yeah, in away. Sat down and had a nice long chat with her in a casino in London about five weeks ago. Andrew was down here with you and the children at the time. It pays to know your enemy, Jan."

"You didn't ... You know, chat her up?"

"Woe no, girl, she ain't that much of a dumb blond. My fancy is that she was just spying out the land for a better deal, or in case the one she's got goes sour on her. I think Andrew's going to be in for a big fat surprise one of these days."

"What, you mean she's a gold digger?"

"Born and bred, Jan. Seen a few of them in my time myself, of that, I can assure you."

"But can't we tell him?" Jan asked.

"Jan, if you don't mind me saying; you married a prize prick. If he can't see what Tracy is by now, there's no way in hell that he's going to believe you or me, if we did try to tell him different. That's of course unless he knows what she's like already, and he's doing all this to take the piss out of you. That would make him one evil bastard. However, I think Tracy is in for the long haul. You said she was his secretary at one time."

"She still is, I think."

"Yeah well, I wonder how much she knows about Andrew's foreign investments or any cash he's got stashed away abroad. You said you thought he had some."

"Yes, but I can't prove it; Andrew kept his financial dealings very close to his chest."

"So you aren't going to get your hands on any of it in a divorce, he's already told you that. Nevertheless, what if Tracy does know where Andrew's money is stashed away. Andrew divorces you and marries Tracy. Then after a year or so, Tracy kicks him out and takes him to the cleaners. You know he can't keep it in his pants, so he's bound to fall by the wayside again sometime." I suggested.

"Why would she get her hands on any of his money, if I can't? If it turns up in the future the court would surely make sure that I got my two pennyworths."

"Tracy's not daft; I doubt she'll get much cash out of Andrew through the courts. No the threat of bubbling Andrew's foreign investments to the taxman and that would be enough to make Andrew very generous." I suggested.

Jan gave me a strange look. "Where do you come up with these stupid scenarios, Tug? She demanded. "Anyway I don't want a divorce from Andrew, I want him back."

It sounded to me that Jan was beginning to lose her cool with me again.

"Believe it or not Jan, it's my job. Anyway, I think you'd do better, to get shot of the wanker, but it's your choice."

"And Chrissie, what do I do about her?"

"Grin and bear it, Jan. Whatever, I'm pretty sure Chrissie will come back to you in the long term. Although I'm no child physiologist."

"I'm worried about losing my children, Tug," Jan said with a long face. But at least it sounded like she was calming down.

"Jan let's take it day by day and see what develops. You just get yourself all tarted up on Saturday evening and we'll call Andrew's bluff."

"Where are we going?"

"The 'Nine Iron Club' for dinner and dancing," I replied, with a smile on my face.

The 'Nine Iron Club' is a rather exclusive restaurant-cum-nightclub, with a dance floor and small casino. It's not too far away from our home town and often they have top-line acts for the cabaret. It's one of those places that, if you have to ask how much it costs to get through the door, you can't afford to go there.

"The Nine Iron Club!" Jan repeated. "But you can't get a table there for trying."

"Unless you are a member or have one of the directors as a close friend," I replied, smiling at her again.

"But ... You can't be a member." Jan had a disbelieving tone to her voice.

"I'm a little better than a member, Jan. I'm a very close friend of the main stockholder of the Nine Iron Club and its associated Golf Club. You might not believe it, but it was my idea to set up the place in the first place."

"You are a dark horse, Tug; I'd never have believed it. Is that what you do, swan around all day with nothing better to do?"

"No Jan, I have a regular job like most folks. Just that my work gives me a little more latitude than most, to pick my working hours. I play golf with some pretty influential people and the Nine Iron Club is just a sideline for them. I pointed out one day that there was nowhere really nice to go around here in the evenings apart from the pubs unless you drove up to town. So, my friends and I came up with the idea of the night club over a round of golf one morning. It was going to be called the 20's Club, for the twentieth Tee, the nineteenth being the restaurant and bar at the Golf club itself. But someone thought the name might be mistaken for the age of the members that place was aimed at, so they settled on for the Nine Iron as in the golf club iron."

I figured it wouldn't do any harm to let Jan know that I wasn't the Hells Angel she seemed to think I was and inform her that I sometimes mixed with some pretty highbrow company.

"Oh, my, the Nine Iron Club," Jan said as she stood up and headed for the door. "I'd better look out something to wear," she mumbled to herself as she went.

"Bye Jan, I'll pick you up at seven, okay?" I said, smiling to myself.

"Yes, thanks. Oh sorry Tug, but you've kind of taken me by surprise. Goodbye, I'll see you Saturday." Jan suddenly remembered her manners.

It looked like I had given Jan more of a shock than I figured I would. She walked right past her car, lost in thought. She was almost out of the forecourt and onto the street before she realised and hurried back to her Disco.

Pete came into the office.

"How'd it go? Looks like you've given the lady something to think about, Tug," he remarked as we watched Jan, making a complete pig's ear of turning the Disco around.

"Yeah, I think she's just realised that I ain't the grease monkey she thought I was. Took the wind right out of her bleeding sails."

"You're not getting sweet on that woman, are you Tug?" Pete asked, "You normally like to keep people in the dark."

"No Pete, but Janet Symonds always liked to look down on everyone. I thought it would be fun to show her that I'm pretty successful in my line, on the quiet."

"You didn't tell about your books, did you?"

"Pete, you know better than to mention my writing, even in the privacy of this office!" I replied angrily.

"Sorry, Tug," Pete said, and then went on to change the subject as quickly as he could.

At exactly seven o'clock on the following Saturday evening. I pulled up outside Jan's house in the Rolls. My usual leather jacket and jeans, discarded for The Full Monty, complete with a bow tie.

As was doing my best Sean Connery impersonation, walking to the front door, I could make out someone -- I figured most likely Andrew and/or Chrissie -- watching me from behind the net curtains of the lounge window. Before I had a chance to press the bell young James opened the door and stood there staring at me with a grin on his face.

"Hello young man, your mother is expecting me?" I said.

"Yes sir, she'll be down in a minute. Won't you please come in?" the boy asked somewhat nervously, I thought.

I was to gather that Jan and her son had planned the next few minutes.

I followed James into the lounge, whereby then Andrew and Chrissie were seated, pretending to be looking at the television. At first, neither appeared to even notice my arrival.

James did invite me to take a seat, but for reasons of self-defence, I decided to remain standing.

"I'll tell mum you're here." the boy said, then rushed out of the room again. I watched the lad take the stairs two at a time.

After Jan's husband stole a glance in my direction and gave me a cursory look over, he then stood up and turned to face me. However, he didn't approach me, if anything he increased the gap between us. I have to assume that that first glance had warned him not to try to get clever.

"So you're the wife stealer?" he eventually said.

I fixed him with my sternest expression. "I think you've made a mistake, sir! I'm not the type of individual who goes about stealing other people's spouses. If however, the lady has been deserted by her husband, then I have to assume that it's open season. Tracy informed me that you're intending to divorce Jan before very much longer anyway, so pray tell me, what are you so concerned about?"

The mention of Tracy and the inference that I'd spoken to her, took both Andrew (and young Chrissie) by complete surprise, as I'd hoped it would.

"What do you know about, Tracy?" Andrew demanded.

"Only that she likes going to the Kat Club on Saturday evenings when you're down here, pretending to play daddy. Likes her drink a bit as well, doesn't she?" I smiled at him.

It was very funny; the poor bugger didn't know what to say in reply. I figured that he must know that Tracy was a regular at the Kat Club because from what I'd learnt, they were frequently in there together. However, did he know that Tracy went there on her own when he was with the children? Andrew's face took on a slightly pinkish hue and I saw him clench his fists. But just at that moment, Jan came into the room, followed by her son James.

"For you my lady," I said handing her another bouquet of yellow roses this time.

"Thank you, kind sir! Jan replied, taking the bouquet from me and handing it to Chrissie, who had stood up as well when her mother entered the room. "Would you please put these in water for me, Chrissie, please? We'd better go Tug; we can't be late for our table at the Iron club."

Chrissie didn't reply, I think she was just as shocked at the sight before us, as I was. Janet looked like a film star going to a premier. I held out my arm, Jan took hold of it and I led her out to the car.

"See you later kids, be good for your father!" Jan called out as we left the house.

"This isn't yours, is it?" Jan asked, looking around the inside of the Rolls as we drove away.

"I've got some good friends Jan, I can lay my hands on just about anything when I need to," I replied.

I thought that was quite clever, I hadn't said whether the Rolls was mine or not, so I couldn't be accused of lying. I just let Jan draw her conclusions.

"You know, you're a real dark horse, Tug. I've just realised that I know virtually nothing about you."

"Not the tearaway that you thought I was at school then, Jan?"

"I don't know. You appear to have many influential friends and more money than I ever expected you to have. I have to ask myself where it all came from though." She asked.

"Would it satisfy you if I told you I got it legitimately, well mostly. You could even call it from gambling!" I replied.

Well, that's not exactly a lie either. I, or rather my publishers, take a gamble that my next book is going to sell well every time they front up cash to me to let them publish one of the buggers. I hadn't had a duff one yet, but nothing was stopping any of them from being a dog and sticking on the shelves one day. Yeah, that's gambling, whatever way you look at it.

"Doesn't sound like a proper way to earn a living to me, and not very reliable," Jan commented.

"I suits me, and I make enough to live the life I want to lead."

"You must do well to be able to afford to take me to the Nine Iron Club."

"I don't pay to eat there, Jan; I told you the place was my idea in the first place. So I get a kind of special dispensation. Free membership there and at the golf club as well. I thought we'd give the driving range a miss tomorrow and play a round of golf instead."

"I think I'd like that. But can you get a Tee time at this late hour?"

"No problem I booked it already, and you better miss the gym tomorrow as well, these six am larks on Sunday mornings are killing me. We'll have lunch at the golf club as well."

The evening went well, there wasn't a top-line cabaret on that night, but it was an enjoyable evening. Jan remarked that we didn't go into the casino, but I told her that I didn't mix business with pleasure. The truth is, there's no fun in winning your own money if you can understand that, but I didn't let Jan in on the secret.

I believe that I need to digress a little here and explain my ... the situation in life. I don't like to talk about it, but sometimes one is forced to. I don't want anyone to get the idea that I'd got where I was at that time on the strength of my writing talent alone. The truth is, I'd always wanted to be a serious author as a child, however, I hadn't exactly had the upbringing that might encourage a literary bent.

My father was a turf accountant by profession. Well, that's what he called himself! Dad was a bookie and a gambler, mostly at dog tracks ... and a decidedly dodgy bookie as well, if you were to ask me. Although, my father was extremely ... plausible character. I never could understand how he always seemed to manage to lay-off most of the bets on the winning dogs, onto other bookie's. Even as a youngster I had it figured that something that wasn't quite kosher was going on there somewhere.

Jean and I didn't have the best upbringing after our mother passed away. Spending many long cold evenings hanging around different wet and windy dog tracks all over the country, watching the mugs give their hard-earned cash away to our father. One thing I did learn from my old'-man though, was that you don't let anybody know how much you're holding in your stash.

Possibly because we'd grown-up in a rented council house, when our father died, Jean and I had been shocked when we learnt the extent of our inheritance. Regretfully my sister had used the greater part of her share -- after buying a nice house -- to finance her first husband's aspirations to follow in my father's footsteps. That proved to be a very big mistake in the long term. That bloke made our father look like a bleeding Saint. He disappeared into thin air with what was left in the bank one night. Although I must admit that Jean always claims she kicked her husband out, some folks suggest that -- fearing Jean's reaction -- the bugger legged it before she discovered that the bank account was empty.

I had been a little cannier and eventually invested my inheritance in property development. i.e. one very exclusive golf club, and its associated business concerns. I wasn't the majority stoke by a long chalk, but I had been the ideas man behind the venture. And of course, via a holding company. I did own the freehold to what had once been a pretty extensive, but an extremely unprofitable farm.

Maybe I should clarify that. After leaving school I started working for my Dad learning the ins and outs of being a bookmaker. And one or two other shady businesses dad was involved with. I didn't take long to decide this wasn't the life for me.

On my eighteenth birthday, I entered the recruiting office and signed up to join the Royal Marines. When dad found out what I'd done he went ballistic calling all the derogatory names he could think of.

When I packed my bags to leave for the Commando training centre at Lympstone (CTCRM) or boot camp as the Yanks call it. Dad was away at some race track up north somewhere. Only Jean was there to see me off

It was hard getting through that basic training. This was where I first met Pete and Geordie we seemed to gel together right from the start. But along with Pete and Geordie, we made it through. A few fell along the way who couldn't handle the intense training. About two-thirds of our original intake made it.

It was a very proud day on that passing out parade when we were awarded that coveted Green Lid (Beret). We marched passed with the Royal Marine band blaring out 'A Life On The Ocean Waves'

Then went to join our units. After a couple of tours of Northern Ireland, numerous training courses. I had reached the rank of Sergeant in 42 Commandos

Just after I had been promoted, I received a phone call from Jean. Dad had suffered a massive heart attack and died whilst doing his thing at a dog track meeting. I went home on compassionate leave for the funeral. Jean and Yvonne dads' solicitor/ business adviser and we suspected girlfriend had sorted out all the arrangements.

I was amazed at the numbers who turned up to pay their respects. Some decidedly dodgy characters amongst them. Standing on the sidelines observing all were several members of the old bill in plain clothing. All standing out like a sore thumb.

After the funeral, Jean and I went to Yvonne's office to read dads will. We were both stunned at the amount that Dad had squirrelled away in cash and investments. I signed over a power of attorney to Yvonne to look after my interests.

Six months after dads funeral I had married my long time girlfriend from my schooldays Laura Joans. On the advice from Yvonne, I kept quiet about dads' inheritance to us.

Then 1982 Argentina decided to invade the Falklands Island in the South Atlantic

So next Maggie Thatcher sent us to kick the Argentineans arses back to Argentina. I kissed Laura goodbye reported into my unit. Then, we're all loaded up on the ships of the Task Force, sailing south to Confront the Argies.

Most of us treated it all as a great adventure. We were singing that song by Cliff Richards and the Shadows

'We're all going on a summer holiday

Going to kick an Argie arse or two '

Once we landed at San Carlos on East Falkland, on 21 May 1982 it was all chaos and confusion. We'd lost most of our helicopters when the Atlantic Conveyor was sunk by Two Exocet missiles.

That left us carrying 80-pound (36 kg) loads and with a three-day Yomp (Your Own Marching Pace) towards Stanley. We were tasked to take Mount Harriet back from the Argies; 3 Para were to take Mount Longdon, 45Commando The Two Sisters.

We were close to our start line at the base of Mt Harriet when suddenly there was a bright flash and loud bang from upfront. We all dived down laying on soggy wet peat. One of the lads had stepped on a mine.

I shouted out **"Stay down don't move! We're in a sodding minefield"** Eventually two engineers came up from the rear and started clearing a way for us to pass through the minefield.

The order came back from the front of the line to get our arses up move forward I needlessly told all the lads to step carefully into the footsteps of the guy in front and pray he didn't step in the wrong place.

We had just reached our start line at the base of Mt Harriet. Then we witnessed one of the most amazing firework displays I have ever seen as HMS Glamorgan pulverised The Two Sisters, HMS Avenger, HMS Arrow and HMS Yarmouth were pulverising Mount Longdon and Mount Harriet, It was dark but the night sky to my left was lit up as those 4 British warships fired almost 800 rounds at the three targets we are attempting to take back from those Argies who were dug in on the upper slopes. The noise from the shells landing from the battleships in the distance was deafening. The Argie positions were being smashed to bits which we hoped would help us a little when it came time to advance up the hill.

I called the lads around "Ok this is it drop your packs stand by, Nobody is to get killed without prior permission, Watkins you welsh perv no sloping off and molesting sheep ok. Ok, we advance by section check weapons and stand by".

Then the Incoming rounds from HMS Yarmouth stopped and then it was time to advance up the hill.

Section by section leapfrogging each other providing cover, we started advancing up the slope dodging boulder to boulder

We were about halfway up when the Argies opened up, on us. Mortar bombs were exploding and tracer fire from machine guns was seeking us out. Pete, Geordie, and a few other lads with us suddenly found ourselves under sustained machine-gun fire from an MG nest about 100 yards to our front. Tracer rounds were bouncing of rocks all around us. We had all dived for cover all trying to bury ourselves into that hard rocky ground.

Geordie was laying close to my left he shouted to me "f@@k this" Then his head exploded spraying me with blood and brains. That's the last I remember. According to Pete and some of the other lads, I had jumped up and charged those Argies like some mad Viking berserker. I took out that machine gun nest.

Next thing I knew Pete and a couple of lads were holding me down wrapping field dressings around my head, then it all went black.

I woke up on the hospital ship the SS Uganda on our way back to the UK. I had been hit by a ricochet bullet bouncing off my head nearly scalping me and a bullet wound to my upper left leg causing extensive muscle damage and narrowly missing the femoral artery.

This was where Pete had saved my life by patching me up, then carrying me, on his back, to the medics who had set up an aid station down at the base of the mountain.

On arriving back in the UK, I was transported to Stonehouse Naval hospital for an extended stay and physiotherapy learning how to walk again. I hadn't heard anything from Laura my wife I had tried phoning. But no luck with that. My sister Jean travelled down to visit but hadn't seen or heard from Laura. It was the second week at Stonehouse that I received an official-looking envelope that I had to sign for.

Opening and reading the contents I was in total shock. It was for the dissolution of marriage. It turned out Laura had cleaned out our joint bank account and buggered off with some Wanker she worked for obviously she had decided to trade up for greener pastures. I phoned Yvonne she told me not to worry she would deal with Laura just concentrate on recovering.

Despite going into a severe bout of depression, I was making progress I could now walk again with the aid of crutches and a sadistic physiotherapist.

Then the second blow of the hammer fell. I was being given a medical discharge from my beloved Royal Marines with a small war disability pension. This was the end of my career in the Royal Marines

I was given an invite to Buck House still shuffling along on crutches where HRH pinned a medal to my chest.

It was whilst I was laying in that hospital bed that I started writing those mushy romance stories. I had been dragged away to be tortured by that physio. I had left my exercise book of writings on my bed.

On return from that torture session, I found Jean sat by the side of my bed reading my scribbling.

"Tug this is looking pretty good it just needs tidying up a bit"

"Hi, Jean, I'm doing good thanks for asking"

"Shut it, less of your lip, Raymond Wilson"

"Seriously Tug this looks pretty good. Let me have a go at it"

"You're welcome if you think it that good take it," I said.

Jean took the two stories I had written edited them, sorted out my bad spelling and punctuation. Then with the help of Yvonne had them published under a pen name and royalties started rolling in. This started my new career as a full-time author.

I was now a civilian spending my time churning out those mushy stories. I had money from my inheritance wondering what else I could do with myself

I ... well, I had aspirations of becoming a gentleman farmer and I'd blown a good part of my inheritance on the establishment.

However, I soon learnt that I wasn't cut out to be a farmer and the venture rapidly deteriorated into financial chaos. Yeah, for a while there, I was that elusive farmer on a bike ... pushbike (or pedal cycle) to be precise.

However after Laura had gone, but before I got around to topping myself or I sunk completely into the quagmire, I encountered some investors ... No, I didn't find them. Yvonne has her finger in all sorts of pies, and they were her marks, and I don't mean that in a nasty way. Yvonne is a solicitor, businesswoman and she keeps her eyes and ears open. She got her commissions from both parties. Yvonne had been a close business associate of my Dad.

Whatever, the golf club came into being remarkably quickly and what's more, Laura can't get her paws on any of it. Nothing like having a good solicitor on your side, even if -- as a type -- you don't like them as people.

I have to admit that I wasn't too enamoured with the majority of our club members and/or clientele of the -- later added --Nine Iron Club, so I rarely visited either establishment myself. Except of course when I wanted (or needed) to make a good impression on someone.

Anyway, back to our night out at the club. After a surprisingly enjoyable evening of dinner and some dancing. All too soon the evening came to an end

It was two in the morning when I brought Corniche to a standstill outside Jan's house. The place was in darkness, except for the light on over the front door.

"Thanks for a lovely evening, Tug. I haven't enjoyed a night like that in years," she said after giving me a quick peck on the cheek. "Everyone treated me like a queen "What did you expect Jan? All the staff know me and always look after my friends - just you wait until we get to the golf club tomorrow."

"Would you like to come in for a coffee?" She asked.

"I don't think that's a good idea, Jan, not with Andrew in there. Anyway, we've got an early start in the morning."

"Early, I thought you said at nine o'clock."

"Jan, it's gone two now, I'll be lucky if I get five hours shuteye by the time I get to bed."

"Yes, I suppose you're right. Goodnight," she said and closed the car door.

I had noted one of the upstairs curtains moved just a little as Jan had got out of the car. I'm not sure why I didn't get out of the vehicle myself and escort her to the door, but for some reason, I chose not to.

Jan went to the door and opened it, turned to give me a little wave, then stepped inside and closed the door behind her.

I just sat there waiting with the window down. I figured I'd hang around for a little while, just in case Andrew turned nasty. After fifteen minutes or so, I'd heard nothing untoward and all the lights in the house had gone out, so I drove home.

I was outside the house at nine the following morning. This time I had the roof down on the Rolls and I was enjoying the morning sunshine. Before I got anywhere near the front door, Jan appeared from around the side of the garage with young James carrying her golf clubs for her.

I took the bag from the lad and placed them in the boot with my own.

"Nice car, bet it cost a fortune," James commented.

"Not that much really, it's a 1980's model. But it drinks petrol like it's going out of style." I replied smiling.

"I'd love a ride in it." The boy very unsubtly hinted.

"We'll see; perhaps I can arrange to be passing when you're going to school one morning," I suggested.

"Coming home time would be much better," James replied. "All my friends would see me in it then."

"Go on with you, go back inside and finish the breakfast your father's cooked you." Jan chided the lad.

"Yuk!" was James' only comment before he ran back around the side of the garage.

"Doesn't he kiss his mother goodbye?" I asked, noticing James failure to do so.

"That's sloppy stuff, to a twelve-year-old, Tug. Now if I was that little blond Vicky Abbot from number 22 that would be a different matter. She's in James's class at school and he's sweet on her." Jan smiled at me.

I filed that piece of information away in my brain for future use.

The day went well, I think. It was Jan's first time on that particular course and I believe her first time using a golf buggy as well. Anyway, she turned in a very respectable round, and I thought that I'd have to look to my game if I played her too often. All right, Jan whitewashed me.

She informed me that apparently everyone had been asleep when she got home the previous evening. However, there were signs that someone had been sitting on the end of her bed. There was also a ring on her dresser as if somebody had placed a wet glass on there. I informed her about the curtain moving as she got out of the car.

"So someone was waiting up until I got home; I hope it was who I want it to be," she said.

"Seems likely, with the glass," I suggested.

We ate a leisurely lunch and then I drove Jan home again. A little earlier than usual for her on Sunday, just in case Andrew wanted to talk about anything. I told Jan to leave the front door on the latch and to set her mobile phone up to call mine with one button press. I'd wait nearby just in case Andrew lost it.

"Oh don't worry, Andrew wouldn't get violent with me," Jan replied.

"Oh no, when you married him you didn't think he'd run around on you either." I reminded her.

"That's different!" she retorted.

"How is it, Jan? What Andrew has been doing to you is not far short of mental torture. That shows his complete disrespect for you. To him, you're nothing more than a chattel at his beck and call. You've no idea how he could react if he thinks you're standing up for yourself."

"You worry too much Tug! Andrew won't hurt me," she said and gave me a quick kiss on the cheek again as I handed over her golf clubs. "See you in the week!" she said, then disappeared around the side of the garage. I spent the next hour parked in a nearby street, just in case.

It was nearly midnight when the telephone woke me; I'd been dozing in a chair. The last thing I remembered was thinking that I should take a shower and get myself to bed early. Still half asleep I fumbled picking the telephone up.

"Tug are you there!" Jan almost screamed down the line.

"Yeah, I was asleep, what's up Jan?" I asked, concerned about the tone of her voice.

"I think Andrew's left me!"

"Jan, you might not have admitted it to yourself, but Andrew left you months ago."

"No, he said he's moving out for good and he's going to see a lawyer about a divorce. He's not going to stay here at the house on weekends anymore. He says he'll have the children up to stay with him in London over the weekends."

118

"I wonder what Tracy is going to say about that?" I chuckled.

I shouldn't have, I know, but I would have liked to have been a fly on the wall when Andrew told Tracy about that plan. But I suddenly realised that Jan was crying.

"Damn it, Janet, stop crying. You're letting him do it to you again!"

"Do what?"

"Torture you! Can't you see the prick's taking the piss out of you yet again? He was annoyed that we went out together over the weekend and he's thrown a bloody tantrum. He thought he had you hanging on a string until he decided what he wanted to do. Now you ... we've forced his hand. Let's wait and see what happens next weekend. I somehow don't think Tracy is going to be too pleased about playing mummy to your two children."

"How do you know?"

"Just trust me, Jan! I told you, I had a long talk with Andrew's Tracy that night, and children aren't on her agenda; she detests the idea of having children around the house. Besides that, Andrew's going to want to know what Tracy was doing talking to strange men in a night club, as well. Everything's going to be very fluid for a while, Jan; just you sit back and wait."

We talked a little more and I think I calmed Jan down a little. After about an hour on the phone, she decided that she was going to bed, so we ended the call.

Monday afternoon I just happened to be passing the school at the end of lessons. I parked the Rolls behind Jan's Disco and got out to talk to her.

"How are you feeling today?" I asked when she finally noticed me standing by her door.

"Sorry Tug, I was in a world of my own." she replied, "I don't know whether we did the right thing; Andrew was furious last night when he left."

"You haven't heard from him today then?"

"No. He said the next I'd hear would be from his solicitor about the divorce. I think he's going to do it, you know."

"I know that you don't want to hear this, Jan; but in my opinion is that that is good news; at least you'll know where you stand. Now give this woman a ring when you get home." I said handing Jan a business card. "She handled my divorce for me and she's shit-hot. Make sure you tell her that I recommended her to you personally and that you suspect that Andrew has assets stashed away abroad."

"But I don't want a divorce Tug, you know that!" Jan replied with an exasperated tone to her voice.

"Then tell Yvonne that you'd prefer to hang on to the bugger. Personally, I think you're potty to even contemplate the idea, Jan; but it's your life. Yvonne is an old hand at this divorce lark, she might well persuade

Andrew that it's cheaper for him to drop Tracy, come back home and be a good boy." I suggested.

"But Andrew's got a top-notch divorce lawyer, he told me."

"That's good Jan because that means the bugger will know all about Yvonne Goldman and he will probably crap his pants when he hears her name."

"She's that good!"

"The best in the country, I can assure you. She doesn't work for just anybody either, only for ... Well, let's just say, that I know that she'll take your case for you, especially if you mention my name."

"Is she another friend of yours?"

"You could say that. Besides my divorce, we've done some other business together. One thing you can be sure of is that Yvonne looks after your interests."

I'd just said that when young Chrissie approached the car. She gave me a look of disgust before climbing into the rear of Jan's Discovery.

"Say good afternoon to Mr Wilson, Chrissie," Jan instructed her.

"Hello!" the girl replied, grudgingly.

Jan caught my eye and raised her eyebrows.

"Hi Chrissie, had a good day?" I asked cheerily, knowing full-well the sort of answer I'd get.

"It just took a turn for the worse!" The young girl replied.

"Touché!" I replied, grinning at her mother. At the same moment, I spotted James standing by my Rolls. He and the young girl with him were looking inside the car. When he saw me watching him James walked towards us.

"That sure is some car you've got there, Mr Wilson," he said to me and then to his mother "Mum can we give Vicky a lift home?"

"Of course we can," Jan replied.

However, I decided to make a different offer.

"Why don't I run you two home in the Rolls?" I suggested.

James and Vicky's eyes lit up. "Can we mum?" he asked.

"I can't see why not," Jan replied grinning at me again. "That's if Mr Wilson has nothing better to do with his time, I'll see you at home, James." Then with a quick wave to her son, Jan started the Disco and drove away. Chrissie, still sitting in the rear seat, glaring at me.

"This way sir and madam," I said, leading the way back to the Rolls where I opened the door and folded the seat forward to allow them access to the rear.

"This is some car, Mr Wilson!" James said after he'd climbed in with his young lady.

"It's Tug, James try to remember that; seatbelts on please."

"Mum wouldn't like me to call you, Tug. She says we have to be respectful towards you." The boy replied.

"Tug is being respectful, if I tell you to use the name, James. You can think of me as a friend."

We drove sedately down the road, taking the longer route back to Jan's street to pass all the local bus stops, where it appeared a lot of James and Vicky's peers were waiting for their own transport home. I was pleasantly surprised that neither James nor Vicky called out to any of their friends, or replied to any of the shouted comments that came from them. In the rearview mirror, I watched the young pair giving the public in general, the royal wave.

"Thank you, that was very kind of you, Mr Wilson," Vicky said as we let her out of the car outside her house. "I hope my mother has seen me arrive home in this."

"Well don't forget to tell her that I'm an old friend of James's mother's, or she'll most likely have a pink fit," I told her.

"Oh, she knows, she saw you with James's mum in it on Sunday. See you tomorrow James." The young girl said and trotted off towards her house.

I slipped the Rolls back into drive gear for the short trip along the road to Jan's house.

"Nice girl you've found yourself there, James." I congratulated him. "Have you asked her out on a date yet?"

"I'm not sure how to." The boy replied.

"That's the easy bit, James. All you've got to say is, there's a good film on at the cinema this week, would you like to come and see it with me?" I suggested.

"No chance, I have to go out with my dad on the weekends, and he'd get all out of shape if I didn't go with him. He's bad enough as it is."

We were at Jans' house by then and she was waiting in the drive for us to arrive.

"I was getting worried, I thought you'd got lost," she said as I stopped the car.

"We had to go the long way round, for maximum exposure." I grinned at her.

"Are you coming in for a coffee today?" She asked. "Give the neighbours something to gossip about."

I accepted Jan's offer -- without informing her that it was apparent that the neighbours were already gossiping -- and followed her inside. Chrissie was in the kitchen as we entered by the back door; she took one look at me and left the room. Neither Jan nor I made any comment.

Within minutes of entering the house, James was on the telephone to a friend about the ride home he'd had in the Rolls. Jan asked him to take his conversation elsewhere so he left the room taking the telephone with him.

"He likes you," Jan said once we were alone.

"I think the fascination is more with the car," I replied.

"You could be right, maybe he's mercenary like his father."

"So you are beginning to see that Andrew has got faults then, besides being an..."

"Don't say it Tug, the children are in the house." Jan chastised me before I'd finish my sentence and for some inexplicable reason, that annoyed me.

"I was going to say 'idiot', Jan Andrew's behaving like an idiot," I repeated to her.

"Oh, I thought you were going to use some of your flowery languages," she mumbled, which was what I'd suspected.

"I think I'd better go," I said, and then I just walked out of the house again.

I hadn't had the coffee that Jan had invited me in for. I'd have been too angry to drink it. Jan had just shown me what her true opinion of me was. She thought that I didn't know how to set a good example in front of children. Some bloody front the woman had; had her husband been demonstrating an acceptable way for a man should treat his wife and family?

Damn, I was angry with Jan. Only, to be honest I can't think why I should have been. Didn't I play the part of a "bad boy" around town to keep folks at arm's length? Looking back now, I wasn't at all sure why I'd got so annoyed with Jan that day.

It was nearly ten days before I saw Jan. I was at Pete's garage having a coffee with the boys again when she came strolling into the workshop.

"May I have a word, please, Tug?" She asked me when she got close enough.

"Sure go ahead," I replied.

"In private, please?" Jan asked.

I looked around, carefully. All of the boys, including Pete, had made a swift withdrawal to the far end of the workshop when they'd spotted Jan approaching. "We seem to be alone."

Jan looked around, kind of furtively. "I was thinking ... Could we go into the office, please Tug?" She asked.

"Lead the way," I said, hopping off the bench.

"I haven't seen you around, lately." She said as I closed the door.

"No, been a bit behind with my work, had some catching up to do, Jan," I replied trying to sound as nonchalant as possible.

Actually, I was dying to know what had happened the previous weekend, but I'd convinced myself, I wasn't going to ask.

"Oh, I thought it was something that I might have said," she said.

"No, I've got a living to earn Jan, just like everyone else. Now was there something important you wanted."

"Well, I was wondering, because I never saw you anywhere over the weekend. We've normally been running into each other somewhere in the last few weeks. I thought you might be avoiding me."

"No, just the pressure of work Jan, I can assure you. How have you and the kids been getting on?" So much for my conviction.

"Moot point. Chrissie has been giving me some real grief. She says that it was us, you and me, going-out together that upset her father. Oh, and by the way, it could be you were right. Andrew didn't take the children home to his flat last weekend, he came down and stayed in a hotel and took them out from there."

"And James?"

"Hmm well, James doesn't seem to give a damn about his father, he keeps asking when you and I are going out again."

I had trouble working out if Jan had said that because young James had asked her, or if she was asking me the question.

"I thought we'd pushed Andrew hard enough for the time being the other weekend. No sense in overdoing it, if you do want him back. What's he done about the divorce he was shouting about?" I asked, quickly changing the subject.

Jan started to laugh. "Oh, that was funny. You were right there as well. I went to see Yvonne on Wednesday and told her the story. Oh when I asked her about how much it was going to cost, she told me that I should discuss the financial side with you - what's that all about?"

"I have Yvonne on a retainer Jan and the contract includes anyone who works for me. Should the divorce go through, Yvonne will force Andrew to cough-up for her expenses. If he chickens-out, we'll figure something out, like putting you on the books for a while. Oh if anyone asks, say that you've have done some research for me. (Maybe that was a truer statement than Jan would ever know.) Yvonne owes me a few favours, so don't worry about how much she's going to cost you."

"Thanks, Tug! Anyway, Thursday last week, some woman from Andrew's solicitors called me and asked me who was going to represent me. When I mentioned Yvonne's name I don't think she believed me at first. I had to repeat it her name twice and then the woman checked the address. Yvonne called me later in the day and told me that Andrew's brief had been in touch and asked to meet with her to discuss the situation. Yvonne says she thinks the guy's worried and she told me that I should refuse to discuss anything about the divorce with Andrew."

"And?"

"Well, Andrew wanted to talk on Sunday afternoon when he brought the children back home. When I asked him what he wanted to talk about, he said the divorce. So I told him, he'd called-in the legal eagles, in the first place; I had no intention of discussing it with him. He went loopy, called me a slut for going out with you and stormed out of the house."

"Good on you, girl! You see he's not happy because he isn't pulling the strings anymore. Now, I know you would rather he gave up Tracy and came back to you. But you might have to let him go, you do realise that?"

"Yes, Yvonne made that quite clear to me. But she said if he does go, it's going to cost him, dear."

"Yeah Yvonne will nail him to the wall, you can bet on it; she knows what she's doing. Did she ask you about the money Andrew have got stashed away abroad?"

"Not that I could tell her very much, but she did ask, yes. She seemed to think that Andrew would find that it might not be as safely hidden as he thought it was. But I don't hold out much hope."

"Don't underestimate Yvonne, Jan. From their reaction, I'll bet Andrew's legal people won't. You see, she doesn't have to find Andrew's money; she can leave that to the income tax people. Tax avoidance is one thing, and quite legal. But tax evasion on the other hand, now that is something completely different. Her Majesty's Tax Inspectors get pissed-off if they think you're hiding something from them, and they will go through Andrew's company accounts with a fine-tooth comb. The threat of that happening should make him a little more generous if you understand where I'm heading."

"What, she'll shop Andrew to the tax people?" Jan said, sounding quite concerned.

"I very much doubt that it will come to that, Jan, and don't worry Yvonne will be very subtle. She just knows how to put the wind up these people. I've seen her in action before. It comes from sorting out a lot of the wayward husbands, who work in the city. They're all into this tax avoidance lark."

Jan and I talked for some time about how I thought Yvonne would lean on Andrew and what the result would probably be, i.e. would he preserve his money and return to playing the loving husband? That I somehow doubted, but I didn't say as much to Jan. Or whether he'd cough up and go through with the divorce; which I thought would most likely be the better outcome for Jan anyway.

But slowly the conversation got around to Jan and me going out on the following Saturday evening. Jan claimed that she wanted to repay me for my help and taking her out to the Iron Club. We finally agreed on dinner at one of the local restaurants, with Jan insisting that she was going to pay.

It was a nice warm spring evening and after the meal, and for want of something better to do, Jan and I took a stroll around town and down by the river. A couple of times Jan slipped her arm in mine just for a few seconds, before she remembered whom she was with, and promptly removed it again.

I've got to admit that it was a comical situation. Two folks, who had never really liked each another, going out together! I won't call our excursions dates; because that was one thing, they were not. Most of the time, more like restrained sparing matches, to be honest. They were subtle, I grant you, but we did spend a lot of our time taking sly little digs at each other. Our school days, coming up in our conversation quite often.

We'd driven into town that evening in Jan's Disco, as I'm not too sure Jan appreciated the look of my Land Rover that I'd turned up in. Remember she didn't know that the Rolls was mine; she'd been under the impression that I'd borrowed it to impress Andrew and I hadn't enlightened her.

Jan invited me in for coffee when we got back to her house and I'd accepted. But I expressed my surprise that Andrew hadn't brought the children home by the time we'd got there.

"He and Tracy have taken the children down the coast, for the weekend; to Brighton, I believe. I think it's a get-to-know -Tracy exercise." Jan explained. "I just hope that they have a terrible time!"

Quite honestly, I didn't think that Tracy would get on very well with the children, and Jan and I sat speculating on what could have happened, for an hour or so. Before I took my leave, Jan told me that she'd be at the driving range in the morning. A definite hint, I thought, that she would appreciate me joining her there.

Okay, so I did turn-up and smash a bucket of balls around with Jan. Some folks might call it practising their driving, but they take their golf a bit more seriously than I do. That's why Jan had beaten me so easily the one time we'd played a round of golf together.

I was only there at Jan's request; I do believe she was missing the children. I think I could understand how she was feeling, and I was the only person she felt could discuss her problems with. So you see, I didn't have much choice other than being there for her.

You've got to understand Jan's character. Having always thought of herself as the bee's knees, she probably couldn't bring herself to open up about her problems to her usual circle of friends.

And my character if it comes to that. I've always been able to handle myself, but by nature, I'm a bit of a soft touch, and I know it. I was quite young when I realised I had to play the hard man or every bugger would walk all over me. At one time in my early twenties, I'd let my guard down and fall in love with Laura. That had resulted in me getting my heartbroken. Since then I'd played the hard man again and kept everybody at arm's length. But when I thought someone needed help, my compassionate side would come to the fore.

Because Jan's husband Andrew was treating her so abominably, that had stirred the compassionate side of my nature. And not forgetting, the interests of my business side of the situation for seconds. I figured that when I got around to writing this little lot up, it would make a pretty good romantic tearjerker. Maybe even a TV movie; I had a friend in Canada who'd turned a couple of my books into pretty successful ones. Okay, rehashed for the American daytime TV. Nevertheless, my story in the first place, so I got my lucrative cut of the take.

Ah there, now maybe you might realise why I don't brag about my writing. Yeah, that's it, I write sloppy romantic novels that are published under the pen names of Isobel Stein and Lily Stockwell. Don't knock it, I'd made a bleeding good living out of it, but I would die of embarrassment if it became public knowledge.

Where were we, I've digressed a bit haven't I? Oh yeah, Jan and I emptied our buckets and then drove out to the Ponderosa to have lunch there. Jan said she was having a little trouble sleeping whilst the children were away with Andrew. I pointed out that they had only been gone two nights, but she informed me that that seemed like forever to her.

We'd almost finished eating when the pub's governor dropped by our table, sitting himself down without a by your leave. I made the introductions, as I knew that was what he was expecting.

"Pleased to meet you, Janet, it's not very often we see Tug in here with a young lady, especially one as beautiful as you."

Surprisingly for me, Jan blushed at Bert's statement.

"Knock it off Bert!" I said "Jan's an old school friend. That's probably stretching the truth a little, we didn't see eye to eye back then. Anyway, there's no budding romance here; we're just catching up on old times." I added before Bert got the wrong idea.

I was looking Bert in the eye, daring him to push his luck. He knew better than to do that.

He smiled back at me. "Well Tug, what I wanted to ask you is, are you going to turn up on Friday night? The marquee's going up this week and we're having our first shindig of the season on Friday, will you be here?"

"Probably, but I can't give you a promise. You know me, Bert; I'm not sure what I'm doing from one day to the next."

"If you don't turn up, the regulars will be disappointed to miss your party piece," Bert replied. "He's quite a star here, you know," he said, turning back to look at Jan.

"Don't tell me – Proud Mary," Jan commented.

"Ah, you've seen our man in action before," Bert replied laughing.

"He sang that same song at every school concert. Tug, you need to enlarge your repertoire a little, you know." Jan suggested smiling.

"Oh, he has," Bert commented, "You know, once he's had a skinful, we can often get 'Nobody's Child' and 'The Last Farewell' out of the bugger as well." George grinned at me. "But then, of course, some bugger gets lumbered with the job of driving him home afterwards. Although Tug's kipped down in the bar here more than once, haven't you mate?"

Yeah well, they were taking the piss a little, I know, but I was used to that by then. Little did they know I ran through 'Dance The Night Away' and 'Achy Breaky Heart' and quite a few other numbers with the boys during their practice sessions. Well, I told you that my house offered a little privacy, and the C & W group, who played at the Ponderosa, rehearses in the coach house quite often during the winter months.

143

I'm not that much of a singer really: well I'd never thought so. But I do seem to have the knack of being able to sound very much like the original artists, you know I kind of do impersonations of them. In sound only, forget about the looks. Anyway, the boys in the band had persuaded me to somewhat enlarge my repertoire during the previous winter, just for the kick of surprising folks.

Someone called out for Bert to handle some problem or the other, probably change a barrel, so he took his leave from us. But not before, telling Jan that she wasn't to be a stranger and making some comment about throwing a rope on me.

"You'll have to excuse Bert, Jan. He and his wife Amie have been trying to get me married off for years." I said once he was out of earshot.

"He seems a very nice man," Jan commented.

"Well he has to be, you know. It's the old mine host thing. Bert is a very old fashioned publican when it comes down to brass tacks. Amie, that's her over there, all cleavage and smiles, she is a wonderful person as well."

Jan looked across at Amie. "Oh my, she must be half Bert's age," she commented in surprise.

"Yeah, she was a young barmaid here when Bert's first wife passed on. She moved in to look after the children to start with, and well, after a few years they got hitched. She's been a good mother to Bert and Stella's kids. She's only a few years older than the eldest, but they all think the world of her. Christ Bert was in one hell of a state after Stella had her heart attack. It was Amie who kept this place together until he came out of it and got his act together."

"Tug, are you trying to prove something to me by telling me that?"

"Yeah, you could say that I am. You see Jan, there is life after a marriage ends or a spouse dies. I thought you should realise that if you do lose Andrew, it ain't the end of the bleeding world."

"Well, if that's the case, how come you've never got married again, Tug?" Jan demanded.

"It's just that I haven't found the right woman yet, Jan; that's all." I smiled back at her.

"In that case, we'd better find someone for you. I know, what about Jemma Wells? I heard she got divorced a couple of years back."

"Christ you're kidding! Jemma Wells was even more of a stuck-up bitch than..." I managed to stop myself before I put my foot in my mouth.

"I was?" Jan completed my sentence for me. "That's what you were going to say, wasn't it Tug?

I didn't answer

"I can't understand you, Tug. You hated me when we lived back home, and I'm pretty sure you don't like me very much now, or the type of person I am and mix with. So just why are you being so nice, so supportive of me?"

"I have my reasons Jan, but I'd prefer not to discuss them if you don't mind."

"But I do mind, I'd like to know why Mr bad-boy Tug Wilson is being so kind to one of his one-time arch enemies. That's what we were in school, wasn't it?"

I had to think quickly. "I don't bear grudges, Jan. What happened all those years ago, is water under the bridge. Life's too short to dislike anyone if you can avoid it. I thought that you needed someone to lean on, so here I am. I'd do the same for anyone, you know that!"

I do believe it worked.

"Yeah, I think maybe you would," Jan said with a smile on her face. "You certainly had us all fooled at school."

"This might sound a little strange to you Jan, but having a bad boy reputation stops you getting into a lot of trouble. Very few kids at that school ever dared to pick a fight with Tug Wilson, you know. And a couple of little taps kept most of the bullies under control."

"Are you trying to kid me that your reputation as a kind of deterrent?"

"Yeah, still is sometimes, believe me! Your husband had second thoughts that evening for a start."

Jan smiled and then the conversation turned back to speculation on how the children were getting along with Andrew and Tracy. Jan once again airing her worries about the children liking Tracy and even maybe preferring to live with her.

"I haven't been the happiest person to be living around lately," Jan said at one point. "If I'm not careful, I could be responsible for driving my children away as well as my husband."

I tried to assure Jan yet again that Andrew had taken a conscious decision to stray, it was most likely nothing that she'd done. Andrew was just one of those characters who used people to his ends.

"Look, Jan, there are lots of people in this world who are like that. They have a conscience, well, we all have! But some people can ignore theirs. All of us can do it sometimes, Christ we have too. Or those con artists would take us for every penny we have. Most of us will walk past charity boxes without putting our hands in our pockets. Blimey if we didn't, we'd be holding charity boxes for ourselves."

"I've digressed a bit, but what I'm trying to say is Andrew doesn't give a damn about anyone, probably not even Tracy either. She's probably fun to be with and makes him feel like a young man again."

"He's trading me in for a newer model?"

"Not even that, Kiddo! Andrew is one of those people who like to think his peers think he's a real man or Jack the Lad. I'll bet he strolls around those clubs thinking to himself how jealous all the guys are of him, having a dolly bird-like Tracy hanging on his arm. Some of them probably are, but others are thinking 'How much is she costing you, Andrew, me old mate? It probably would have cheaper to use an escort service in the long run son!' That's all Tracy is, and one day Andrew is going to discover that.

"Andrew doesn't care about the money side of things; at least he won't until Tracy puts the screws on him. Moreover, she will do that one day, believe me, I know her sort. She dresses sexy for him, sucks his ... Um, and goes down on him at the drop of a hat. She would probably convince him he's the greatest lover in the world, even if he is useless in bed. Christ, I'll bet the little slut would climb into bed with his clients if he asked her to. It strokes Andrew's ego to think he's running things and he believes that makes him a real man."

"But I do those things for him, I always have. Well, I don't think I'd let his clients bed me, you have to draw the line somewhere."

"You don't get it, Jan. You're what, thirty-six the same as me? Tracy is twenty-two or three, or at least she claims to be about there somewhere. Seen the world a bit that girl, and could be she's a lot older and has just worn better than most. Some girls have the knack of doing that: mind she could have just started very young.

"Anyway, what I'm trying to say is, Andrew doesn't give a monkey at the moment. He's getting his end away and he believes that all his contemporaries think he's a stud. His ego is stroked and his conscience has gone out the window."

We chatted on for a while longer and then Jan drove me back to her place to collect my car. I turned down her offer of coffee, which was lucky in a way because Andrew came around the corner in his car with the children as I pulled away. It was enough that he saw that Jan hadn't been alone for the weekend. Possibly better that he didn't see whether I'd carried an overnight bag out of the house or not.

Jan and I had arranged to meet the following Saturday for lunch. I told her I couldn't say any earlier in case I did go to the Ponderosa on Friday evening. I'll admit I do have to have a few before I can work up enough courage to get up on the stage. Yeah well, I'm sure that -- as most people seem to do -- I sound much better after I've imbibed a few bevvies

Whatever, after lunch Jan and I thought we'd probably catch a matinee or something in the afternoon, depending on the weather.

Because I received no panicking telephone calls from Jan late on Sunday evening, I figured Andrew or the children hadn't dropped any unpleasant surprises in her lap when they got into the house.

The week went by, without me hearing from her, so I assumed everything was as fine as it could be. Friday night I got to the Ponderosa around six-ish and ate there. I chatted with the boys as they set up. Well not set-up really, while they enjoyed their warm-up pints.

Anyway, we discussed the numbers that I might join in on later.

A little after the boys started playing, my cousin Pete turned-up with his wife and family and shortly after that, his boys from the garage arrived with their opposite numbers. There was quite a crowd of us there that night; I thought it was because of it being the first shindig of the summer. It never occurred to me that news of my extended repertoire might have leaked out.

Pete and the boys kept me talking and supplying me with beer so -- until half eight when the crowd started chanting "TUG, TUG, TUG." -- it hadn't registered exactly how large the audience had become.

With my usual feigned reluctance, I headed for the stage, Amie passing me the Stetson I'd bought on my one trip to the States some years before, as I went. That thing dropping on my head always had brought a cheer, as it signified I was in singing mode. When I took it off again, everyone knew I would sing no more, that evening.

Climbing up onto the makeshift stage, one of the guys handed me my battered old acoustic guitar. His checking the tuning of it had set the gang chanting "TUG, TUG, TUG," in the first place. I know they all expected me to sing "Proud Mary" but the first words from my mouth as I leant towards the microphone were "Put your sweet lips a little closer to the phone!" The bloody crowd went wild, I looked over at the table where Pete and gang were and was surprised to find that Jan was occupying the seat I'd so recently vacated. So surprised that I missed a few notes on the guitar, but I doubt anyone noticed or could even hear.

They got "Proud Mary" next. Then we did a couple more numbers from my new repertoire including 'The Last Farewell' by Roger Whitaker all culminating in "Dance the night away!" Okay, an electric organ doesn't quite give the same kind of sound as a few trumpets, but I doubt anyone noticed that either.

Whatever, it was hit with the crowd, and it looked like everyone was up on their feet and dancing, a lot of them trying line dancing in amongst the picnic tables that Bert had out in the paddock. I was taking my leads from the boys, two of whom were singing with me on that one; they just kept the song going for god knows how long. Much longer than the four minutes or so it normally takes to sing. However, that's show business "When you've got 'em going, keep the buggers going!" Mike the group's leader always says.

The next thing I realized was that Jan was dancing right in front of me, so I put my microphone back on its stand and jumped down to join her for a while. That is until I thought the number had gone on long enough when I returned to the stage.

After all that excitement, we gave them "Nobody's Child" to quieten things down a bit and give the audience a chance to rest. Then I sang a couple more numbers before taking a break myself. Jan collared me as I crossed the area of crushed grass that served as the dance floor and we danced the next number together. I was amazed at how happy the woman looked. But then

I needed a sit down myself, and another pint or two. Oh, and I had to make a short diversion, to make way for the liquid as well.

I told Jan I was surprised to see her there and she informed me that she enjoyed C & W music. Besides Andrew had taken the children for the whole weekend again, and she didn't fancy spending the evening in the house on her own. We listened to music and danced to a couple more numbers. Not what you'd call together really, kind-a line dancing. Not easy on uneven ground like that, when most folks - including us - didn't have much idea what we were supposed to be doing anyway, but great fun.

All too soon for my liking really, someone started the crowd chanting Amie. That was for Amie Bert's wife. Anyway, I knew the score and very soon Amie was pulling me from my seat.

Amie is a wonderful person, but she can't sing for nuts! What's more, she knows it. However, a couple of years before when Amie had drunk a few more lemonades than she should have done one evening. She had made the mistake of getting on the stage and trying to sing "Another Somebody Done Somebody Wrong Song", a favourite of hers. Poor Amie got herself in a right old 'two-an'-eight', so - having had a few too many myself and being the mug that I am as well – I'd taken pity on the woman and jumped up there with her and we'd sung it as a duet.

From that evening on, Amie had been forced to embarrass herself every time they held one of those shindigs. Not that Amie minded getting up there. She treated it as a bit of fun. It becomes a bit of a game. One time Amie hid in the ladies loo and refused to come out until some bright spark shoved a microphone through the window then stood outside and told the band to start playing. Amie relented and went on stage but -- if I was there -- she always dragged me along as well. After that night, it became a regular part of the evening's entertainment.

To be honest, because just about everybody knew the song and joined in. I doubt whether many people heard that Amie and I were singing at all.

Anyway, back to that night. Amie dragged me up on stage – me playing at being reluctant once again – and Amie sang (?) the opening line, then the band and I joined in. Amie and I normally shared a microphone for that song, so I was taken a little by surprise when she reached out, and took one of the others off of its stand, then moved over to the side of the stage.

When I looked across to see what she was getting up to, my duet partner had got down of off the stage and was all cosied up to Jan, who was by then sharing Amie's microphone. I do believe somewhat reluctantly, but Amie had never been one to take no for an answer.

Then I noticed that Amie was gesturing with her free hand to Pete and his wife, who was standing nearby. Jan suddenly found herself unceremoniously hoisted up and dumped onto the stage. For a moment, the poor woman looked like a rabbit caught in a car's headlights at night. But very quickly Amie was on stage beside her and she guided Jan over to where I was standing.

Amie gestured for Jan to share the microphone that I was using, so I moved back to the side a little to give her room. Then Amie shot-off to join the lead-guitarist whose microphone she'd stolen for her little excursion. The song over Jan thought that she was going to get down again, but someone shouted encore. I hit the first line again and the band joined in, but this time Amie didn't. Out of the corner of my eye, I saw Amie telling the audience to sing quietly. Well, I think she was and most of the audience assumed that was what those weird hand signals she was making meant. That left Jan and me singing the song as a duet. I was surprised that Jan had such a good voice, even more, that she knew all the right words. Her voice worked perfectly with mine on that particular song, or so I was assured later. You don't hear the same as the audience does, when on stage.

I think when Jan realized they were listening to us sing, instead of trying to drown us out, she began to get a little nervous and started to falter. But lead guitarist Mike stepped forward and whispered something to her, she gave him a quick smile and nod, then turned towards me and continued. Very soon her nervousness was gone and we finished the song together.

"Janet Symonds, ladies and gentleman," I said into the microphone, and everyone broke out in applause.

Jan smiled, nodded and waved, feeling very self-conscious I think and then tried to leave the stage. But I had my arm around her waist, so she couldn't getaway. She'd got into that song so I thought I'd see what others she knew. Oh, I didn't ask her, I just called the number to Mike. All the songs we do have numbers, so if we are going to do a set we can just say 1.6.13 and all the guys know what the next few numbers are going to be.

"I can't believe I just did that!" Jan said with an excited smile on her face as we returned to the gang.

I've got to admit that I was way past the staggering stage by that time and just collapsed into my seat. In consequence, I can't reliably report what I said to her. Something along the lines of "You did well, Girl!" I suspect.

To be honest, the rest of the evening is a bit of a blur to me. All I can recall is getting out of Jan's Discovery back at my house at some unearthly hour of the morning. After I insisted that I could make it to the door unaided, I watched Jan drive away.

However, at the crack of dawn on that Saturday morning, she was back hammering on my front door. Alright about half-eleven, but bear in mind the quantity of 'falling down water' I'd consumed the night before. Which for some inexplicable reason was much more than I usually drink by the way. Anyway, believe me, half-eleven is the crack of dawn, or at least it feels like it.

I staggered downstairs and opened the door; then probably glowered at Jan through bleary eyes. I don't think I said anything to her. Jan frowned back at me.

"God you look like shit, Tug!" she commented, before pushing past me and setting out in search of my kitchen.

Well, although her children had, Jan had never been inside my house before, so she had to find it herself.

"Err, what are you doing here, Jan?" I asked, following her.

At first, she didn't reply, however, she did put the kettle on and began searching through my cupboards. However, she discovered the ground coffee first and then went in search of the coffee maker.

"Jan?" I repeated.

Placing the coffee machine on the worktop, Jan looked at me with an expression that I can only describe as disdain on her face. I'd seen that expression many times since I'd first met the woman in our early teenage years.

"If you recall we have a lunch date today and there's no way I'm taking you anywhere looking like that, Tug."

"I thought the general idea was the man took the woman to lunch," I replied, trying to sound funny, I think, even with a hangover.

"With the amount of booze you poured down your throat last night, you aren't driving anywhere today Tug, that's for bloody sure. Blimey, a police officer would probably smell you coming if you got behind a steering wheel. Right, a couple of mugs of strong black coffee should at least get you to wake-up. Then you can enjoy a nice cold shower and try to get both your eyes looking in the same direction.

"Tug, you were really good on that stage last night, you had all those people eating out of your hand, but you really mustn't drink that much alcohol, it's not good for your health!"

"Oh come on Jan, as if you care about my health!"

"Of course I do, Tug. You care about me ... even if it's just because you think my story might make a plot for one of your novels. I use the term lightly, I might add. Any way you do care and that's what's important."

"What did you just say?" I asked wondering if my ears had just deceived me.

"That I care about your health, Tug."

"No, besides that, you said..."

"Oh, I suspect that you're planning to try to use my story in one of your books. Well yes, that always has been pretty obvious. Well, it was to me, once I discovered that you write for a living."

"But what makes you think that?"

"Stick to romances Tug, you'll never make a good detective writer. Firstly, you appeared on the horizon like a Knight coming to the rescue of a damsel in distress. Secondly, for someone who's always hated my guts since we were at school, you showed a little too much concern for the predicament I found myself in. You asked too many questions and were much too keen to help. And you researched Tracy a little too well as well.

"And lastly you sat in your car typing on your computer for hours on end, while you were supposedly clandestinely spying on me; only a professional writer is going to do that sort of thing.

"And besides all that, I have a curious son; he crept up and watched you typing one day. You were so lost in your little world that you didn't even notice him. Then add to that, several copies of the same particularly sloppy romance novel, written by one 'Isobel Stein' stashed away in the glove box thing in the back of your Rolls Royce. Not being a parent you possibly wouldn't realise that children get into everything."

"What makes you think that it's my Rolls Royce anyway, Jan? I told you I borrowed it from a friend. Perhaps, she or he is Isobel Stein."

"Stick to romances, Tug. Pete keeps the garage's work diary on his desk in the office, there was no mistaking the words "Tug's Rolla"; you had it booked in for a service, I believe."

"Bugger," I replied. "Now look, Jan; I don't like to publicise the fact that I'm an author. Doesn't quite fit with the public persona."

Jan giggled. "Don't worry, your secret's safe with me!"

"But what about your son."

"I have his promise, you can trust James to keep his mouth shut, Tug; he likes you. He'll do nothing to upset you on purpose. His street-cred went through the roof when you drove him and Vicky home from school that day. He's hoping for a repeat performance in the future."

"If he keeps his mouth shut, tell him I'll chauffeur him and Vicky on their first proper date."

"It's a little too late for that, Tug; he took her to the cinema one day last week. They had a teacher-training day. I played chauffeur, but to you goes the credit for giving him the impetus to ask Vicky out on that date.

"Now get this down you and let's see if we can sober you up enough, to enjoy lunch; I'm paying."

Jan virtually poured the first mug of coffee down my throat, while she was pouring out the second I retrieved a couple of paracetamol from the cupboard. Then I took the mug from her and retreated upstairs to my room.

To be honest I still wasn't feeling too clever when I eventually came down again. Well, I'm sure many of you will have experienced the odd hangover. However, Jan declared that I passed muster.

To be completely honest, Jan appeared to sound a little too much like my sister Jean, when she chastised me for imbibing more than was good for me. The chastisement wasn't so much done with words, more with facial expression and body language.

Much to my surprise, I found Jan in my study. At first, sight surveying my gardens, however, I suspected already having perused the bookshelves in there, which I'm afraid held copies of every one of my literary ... endeavours. No the word 'works', infers a much higher calibre of publication.

However, Jan's first comment was to sing my gardens' praises. She looked quite deflated when I implied that her accolade was misplaced and all credit should be directed at the old-boy who acted as my gardener.

So then, she started to sing my home's praises. Honestly, I couldn't have come up with so many different things to make nice comments about it, if I tried. Although Jan hadn't been inside my house before ... well, it's big, but it's nothing special.

Eventually, I realised that Jan was procrastinating. So I took hold of her arm and dragged her back into the kitchen. There I gently shoved her into a chair and poured out two more mugs of coffee.

"Okay, Jan; come along, tell daddy what's eating you?" I asked, having seated myself opposite her.

After staring back at me for a couple of minutes in silence, Jan started to go on about how exhilarated she'd felt the night before, standing on that stage. And of course, telling me how good an entertainer I was. However, gut instinct told me that wasn't actually what was on her mind.

"Cut the crap, Jan. What's got up your arse so much?" I demanded.

"You do have a charming turn of phrase, when you want to, Tug," she replied.

"Jan Symonds, something's got you in a right two-an'-eight today. Now, what is it?" I demanded again.

"Alright if you must." She said, then reached over and withdrawing an A4 manila envelope from the handbag - - she'd dumped on the table when she first arrived -- pushed it towards me.

"You were right, he's almost conceded defeat. That's Andrew's proposed terms for our divorce."

I would have liked Jan to explain herself further, but thought I'd better look at what she was showing me first before I asked any questions. From the envelope, I extracted a large file of papers. Skimming through I confirmed that they were an outline proposal for the dissolution of Andrew and Jan's marriage. What shook me was financial settlement Andrew Had offered Jan. Put it this way, money ... or the lack of it, would never be a hindrance to Jan enjoying her life after the divorce.

However, there was one obvious sticking point, the children. Andrew wanted full and exclusive custody of both of them.

"Yvonne has seen this yet, Jan?" I asked.

"No, Andrew left it with me last night when he picked up the children. That's why I went to the Ponderosa last night looking for you. I needed a shoulder to cry on; someone to console me. However, once I got there I found something I wasn't expecting to find. I discovered that life can still be fun. So I'm no longer frightened of what's going to happen after I have got the cheating bugger out of my life. Mind you, I suspect that he's going to put up one hell of a fight over the children, the sod needn't think he's going to get sole custody of my children without a bloody fight."

"Jan, you seem to have done an about-face on me. What happened to the 'I love my husband, and want him back', stance?"

"I'm not sure, Tug; country music maybe. Anyway, a wise man once told me, that when some bastard tries to ... take the piss out of me, I shouldn't just stand there and let it happen."

"Oh yeah and who told you that?"

"Well if you don't know, I'm not going to tell you, Tug. Think about it, that's not my choice of words, is it?"

"Ah, so I'm going to take the can if it all goes belly up, am I?"

"No, Yvonne is; she assured me last week that we had Andrew by the..."

"Short and curlies," I suggested.

"I'd have thought you'd say, balls, Reg."

"I can do ... refined speak, when I wish to, Jan."

"So I see. But all I've got to do now is pray that Yvonne can scupper Andrew's child custody aspirations."

"If anyone can, it's Yvonne. You're in the best of hands with her. I'm just trying to understand your sudden change of ... perspective, Jan.

I told you you've convinced me that there is life after divorce. You stood me on a stage last night and got all those people applauding me. God Tug, I wouldn't have had the nerve to do that six months ago. It was always Andrew getting the ovations at those conventions and stockholder meetings. I was the meek little supportive wife he used to drag along with him."

"Used to?" I queried.

"Yeah used to. It took me long enough, but I now realise that he didn't stop taking me along because of the children. He's been taking his bed partner with him for several years now."

"Ah, the delectable, Tracy."

"And probably Sonya, the little tart he had working for him before her. God Tug how was I so blind?"

Jan and I did get out to lunch, eventually. However, she kept switching between a very confident about-to-become a divorcee and worrying that Andrew was somehow going to get full custody of their offspring. Made for an interesting and somewhat confusing day. At any one minute, I wasn't quite sure if Jan was going to be grinning like a Cheshire Cat or next biting my head off. Yes well, we did exchange some heated words during the day, but generally about nothing of consequence. Hey, it was like being out with my sister, or even Laura, but at the wrong time of the month.

On Sunday after we'd retrieved my Landy from the Ponderosa, we went for a round of golf again, which seemed to keep Jan's mind off the child custody question. However, I think Jan purposely thought about Andrew whenever she teed off. Did wonders for the length of Jan's drives, but didn't work so well when it came to the direction the ball travelled in. I think I gave more balls up as lost that day than I'd ever done, and we walked bloody miles searching for the buggers.

"Tug, you couldn't do me a favour and collect the children from school today, could you?" Jan asked when she called me around Tuesday lunchtime. "I've got to attend a council of war with Yvonne this afternoon."

"Of course Jan, but am I the best candidate? Chrissie won't be too pleased I'm sure. And what should I do with them anyway, take home or back to my place."

For some reason, Jan giggled.

"McDonald's would probably be the most diplomatic and should keep Chrissie's lip in check anyway. Then if I haven't made it there myself, probably your place, the children haven't got a key with them. There are other people I could ask, Tug, but they are liable to ask the children too many questions."

"Your wish is my command milady. I just hope I live to tell the tale. I fear Chrissie's tongue is going to prove to be as sharp as her mother's at her age."

"I'll treat that comment with the disdain it deserves, Tug."

"Regretfully the truth always hurts, Jan!"

"Thank you, Tug. I will see you when I get there. Wish me luck!"

I decided that the Rolls would the appropriate mode of transport. Even Chrissie shouldn't get too out of shape about travelling in that.

James and Vicky found me before I had even started looking for them, but then I had to send them off to locate Chrissie. It was with marked reluctance and a sour expression that James dragged his sister to the car. That face got even longer when I informed the pair that we were going to eat at McDonald's because their mother was held-up at a meeting. Mind you, Vicky didn't look too pleased either when James sat in the front passenger seat and left her in the back with a sulking Chrissie.

Things got slightly more complicated when James asked if Vicky could accompany us to McDonald's. Of course, I didn't refuse, but it did mean I would have to speak to her mother to get her permission; but I'd assumed that I'd have to drive the child home anyway.

Yeah well, the curiosity on the woman's face had to be seen to be believed. However, she was quick enough to give her consent for Vicky to join us. That Rolls Royce has strange effects on people. Think about it, the woman didn't know me from Adam.

We'd just settled at a table, Chrissie still looking decidedly unhappy and bored out of her mind, when James asked me.

"Mr Wilson, what's Bendon?"

"I'm sorry James, I haven't got the foggiest idea."

"Bendedham!" Chrissie barked, correcting her brother.

The first noise, except for a few grunts, the child had emitted, since she'd arrived at the car. But something about the way she pronounced the word made me ask,

"Ah just a minute, are you sure you don't mean Benenden?"

"Yes that's it," James replied. "Benendon."

"No Benenden." I corrected the lad. "It's a very swish girl's boarding school somewhere in Kent, I believe. What makes you ask?"

But when I looked, the lad and his sister were staring at each other with expressions of horror on their faces.

"Hey, what gives?" I asked.

"What if I was to ask you, what Malvern reminds you of, Mr Wilson?" Robert said after a long silence.

Being a complete prune and completely oblivious to both children's concerns, I blurted out.

"A town in Wiltshire." Then still failing to understand the significance of the child's first question, I added. "And the site of prestigious co-educational boarding school."

So there I was sat in the middle of McDonald's with a ten-year child who despised me and who was suddenly bawling her eyes out. That kinda caught me off-guard and I wasn't sure what I was supposed to do at that point. Luckily, young Vicky did appear to know how to handle the situation. Well, she had more idea than I anyway.

The following thirty minutes or so were ... well, bedlam best describes it. Although luckily for me, young Vicky calmed Chrissie down eventually. I learnt from James that over the weekend his father and Tracy had been discussing something neither he nor his sister understood. However, they did pick-up a few -- what they thought was -- place names and they assumed that the adults were talking about living there after their parent's divorce.

However, the misheard or mispronounced list of place names James came out with, (or most of them) were the locations of Public Boarding Schools as far as I was aware. I have to assume the other place names were so mangled that they just didn't ring any bells in my memory.

Although his sister was still upset, James handled the information like an adult. Not that he was best pleased, but he hadn't wanted to leave his mother anyway. His reaction was to ask me how he could ensure that he didn't have to go to live with his father. I don't think the lad was impressed when I told him that that question fell beyond my expertise. However, I could assure him that I'd do whatever was in my power to keep him living with his mother.

"What about me?" Chrissie demanded, an instant after I'd spoken.

I hadn't been aware the child had stopped crying and was paying attention to what I'd been saying to her brother.

"Chrissie, you're mother doesn't wish either of you to leave her. If you wish to remain living with her, then the same goes for you as well. You can count on me to do everything I possibly can to keep you all staying together."

"Why?" Chrissie ... demanded. Okay not as firmly as she could have done, but there was no doubting the child's sentiment.

"Chrissie, your mother and I have been friends since we were at school together. Okay, not as good friends as your brother and Vicky here are, but friends none the less. We can even argue with each other, without bearing malice."

Okay, not exactly the truth, even by that time Jan and I were more akin to sparring partners than friends, but you get my drift.

James felt he had to clarify my little speech for his sister before she even queried it. I believe that was the point that I realised exactly how far out of my depth I was, with children.

I think I was still struggling with the explanations of my and their mother's friendship when relief finally arrived in the shape of the woman herself. Boy was I pleased.

Not for long, though as Jan threw me some withering glances, as Chrissie fell back into wailing mode. The three females went into a huddle on one side of our table, while James and I tried to look intelligent on the other.

Eventually, the clique broke-up and it appeared to have been decided that Jan would take Chrissie home, while I chauffeured the lovebirds, James and Vicky.

I wasn't looking forward to getting back to Jan's place. I'd pulled a booboo with the boarding school revelations, and I knew it. Where children are concerned there are times when you should say as little as possible, and I had not realised I should have kept my bloody mouth shut.

Oddly, once James had dragged me into the house; neither Jan nor Chrissie appeared to be upset about my misdemeanour. It seemed that I'd suddenly become Chrissie's favourite uncle. If the uncle is the best way to describe it. Gone was the long face and the implied daggers, to be replaced by sweet smiles and polite conversation.

Although I have to admit that, the child was scraping the bottom of the barrel when it came to conversation. I believe that she thought she had to say something nice to me, but she didn't know what to talk about. It got quite embarrassing until Jan asked the children whether they had any homework from school. I had to wonder if young Chrissie was usually so keen to do her homework; a relieved expression swept over the child's face and she was gone in a flash.

Jan and I retired to her kitchen where we hoped -- once the door was closed and the children would not overhear us. She briefly described her conference with Yvonne, who had somehow managed to apply a pressure on Andrew to force him to make that generous offer, in that divorce proposal. However, Yvonne seemed to believe she had the wherewithal to persuade Andrew to increase that offer even further.

What's more, Yvonne had ideas about the child custody situation that she thought a Judge would go for. Basically to suggest the court that they let the children decide which parent they wished to live with.

That was why Jan had not been upset with me that evening; and she realised that silly sod Andrew and his stupid Dolly Bird Tracy, had effectively shot themselves in the foot by talking about boarding schools within earshot of both children the previous weekend.

Over the following few months, I didn't see Jan that often, at all. There was a motive behind this, which Jan appeared to understand. If they had any sense, Andrew's legal people would probably be having Jan watched, at least some of the time; there was little point in adding any strings to Andrew's bow.

Yeah okay, sometimes I'd pop into the driving range of a weekend to see if she was there. However, when she was, it was a much more in control of her emotions Janet, who appeared to be able to select any of the target markers and then drop her ball right on it. It was obvious to me that if we ever played a round of golf together again, there would be no wager that was for sure.

Jan did phone me quite often, more frequently when she had received good news from Yvonne about the divorce. And just a couple of times Jan asked me to collect the children from school again when she had meetings with Yvonne. Usually, I took all three terrors to McDonald's and we were all getting along like a house on fire by that time. Young Chrissie would sit in the front passenger seat of either the Land Rover or the Rolls and make polite, obviously carefully thought about, conversation. It would be more like a question and answers game, but I have no idea what the child was attempting to achieve.

Jan never joined us at McDonald's but would telephone when she was about to arrive home. Just a couple of times I took all three children back to my own house because Jan was late and she would collect them from there. However, I wasn't too enthusiastic about doing that, for reasons that should be obvious. We live in these weird times.

I enjoyed a couple of lunches with Yvonne that summer, to discuss my own business. She could not say too much about Jan's divorce because it had nothing to do with me. However, I got the idea that someone on her staff had somehow led a member of Andrew's legal team to believe that a whole raft of Jpegs was in existence. No, not of Andrew and his floozy, but Andrew's private papers; taken by his wife several years earlier when she'd become aware that he was banging his previous secretary Sonya.

When I pointed out to Yvonne, that Jan had only recently come to the supposition that Andrew might have been banging that Sonya bird, Yvonne smiled and said,

"Yes Tug, but Andrew doesn't know that, does he? I just had to make sure that Jan knew how to smirk at the appropriate moment. Nothing is more effective at destroying a cheater's bravado than leading them to believe you were aware of something they thought you didn't know."

"Sounds complicated to me Yvonne," I commented.

"Tug, you create similar scenarios in your novels all the time."

"I've never actually thought of them as novels Yvonne, more wanders through an imaginary world where almost everyone has good intent. Not very true to life, anyway."

"Not the world I live in then, Tug. Anyway, Jan's husband has no idea what we have on him and he's scared out of his wits. He asked Jan to take him back, but she turned him down flat. Seems like your Jan has finally put the trousers on."

"Not my Jan, Yvonne; I'm not even sure how I got involved in all this. There was no love lost between Janet Symonds and me when we were at school together. I couldn't abide the woman ... or girl as she was then."

"Oh, I see! I'd assumed your interest was more of the unfulfilled, could have been, childhood romance type, Tug." Yvonne smiled.

"Yvonne, after Laura, do I look like the sort of idiot who'd get himself emotionally involved with another woman. Bloody tiger at that; my god but the woman does scrubs-up well."

"Ah, you noticed that then, Tug."

"Who wouldn't, Yvonne? Damn the woman always did have a presence even when we were at school, but we never exactly saw eye to eye about anything. You know we still have our moments, but that's possibly down to the strain that Jan's been under. Generally, I think she's mellowed with age. Even goes as far as apologising to me nowadays. That's how I got involved in her troubles really, she approached me and apologised after we'd had an altercation over a punctured car tyre."

"Whatever floats your boat, Tug? I seem to have got hold of the wrong end of the stick; I imagined that there was a budding romance in the offing."

"No chance Yvonne; it's just muggings, Tug, falling for a sob-story again. I've hardly clapped eyes on Jan since her old' man raised the flag of truce."

"It was more akin to unconditional surrender Tug. Jan's been in the driving seat ever since if I could only get the woman to understand that fact."

After that, the conversation got back to the contract Yvonne and I was supposed to have been discussing that day.

As that summer went on, I became aware that Jan had been visiting the Ponderosa on the odd Friday evening. Look I was in the habit of going there myself, but not as often as most people seem to assume. My favoured pastime is ridding Bonnie, often a lot faster than I should. However, I'm no fool! Fast motorcycles and alcohol do not make good bed partners. Consequently, a lot of the time I have to forgo one pleasure in favour of the other. Besides, I don't write well when I'm either pissed or suffering from a hangover.

Whatever, on the odd occasion I had popped into the pub, Amie and Bert both went out of their way to inform me that Janet Symonds had been up on the stage with the band a couple of times during the season. They also hinted that my many so-called fans had remarked upon my lack of presence.

I did make an appearance at the Ponderosa on the final night of the summer season -- before the marquee came down for the winter -- but Jan wasn't there that evening. I got the idea into my head that Jan had been going to the Ponderosa on Friday evenings when Andrew took the children away for the weekend. Although we were still meeting at the driving range on the odd Sunday morning, she'd never mentioned the Ponderosa to me at all.

So it was some surprise a few weeks later that I looked up from my keyboard one afternoon. The band had borrowed the coach house that particular day to rehearse. I think I noted a change of tempo in the music -- that I could just about hear -- and that first broke through my writing haze.

Whatever I suddenly became aware of a face staring at me through the window. On closer inspection, I realised that it was Jan's daughter Chrissie who was making funny faces at me.

Wondering what she was doing in my garden, let alone at my house, I went over and opened the French doors.

"Hello Chrissie, what are you doing here?" Was the obvious question to ask?

"Hi, Uncle Tug," she replied, with a sweet smile.

So different from the looks the child had given me when we'd first encountered each other. Moreover, I can't put my finger on exactly when I'd morphed from Mr Wilson into Uncle Tug, either. Whatever, the child went on.

"I'm here with mummy, watching her rehearse!"

That revelation took me completely by surprise. The lads had never mentioned Jan to me personally since that first night that -- at Amie's insistence -- she'd joined me on the stage.

I think I was struck dumb and found myself standing there watching the 10-year-old as she wondered around my study; having a damned good nose if you ask me.

"You have a nice garden here Uncle Tug, but you still haven't put a swing in that tree."

Chrissie was reminding me that I'd said that it would be a great place to hang a swing, on one of her previous visits. Then she sat in my office chair and swung around on it a couple of times, before bringing it to a stop so she could look at my monitor screen.

"What are you doing?" she asked.

As quick as a flash, I hit the monitor off switch, while frantically trying to recall if there was anything that a child shouldn't be reading on the page I was rewriting. Of course, some of my stories have a modicum of titillation in them. It doesn't matter what way you look at it, sex sells!

"Oh, it's just work, Chrissie, nothing exciting. How long has your mother been singing with the group?"

"Oh, she only jams with them sometimes at present." -- That statement didn't sound like it came from a child, I had to assume Chrissie had overheard an adult make it -- "But Uncle Mike keeps asking her to be the band's lead singer. Mummy says she won't earn very much money, but it will get her out of the house some evenings. Vicky's mother is going to sit with me and James."

"James and I." I corrected Chrissie, but she ignored my comment.

"Uncle Peter says mummy can go home early from the garage when she wants to sing with the band."

The news was coming at me almost quicker than my mind could take it in. Janet Symonds was going to be the group's lead singer and it sounded very much like she was working -- or was about to start work anyway -- for my mucker Pete at his garage. In the office, I suspected, but knowing Pete, more like as eye candy designed to keep the punter's minds off their bills.

I have no idea where my mind went for a while, but eventually, I realised that young Chrissie was sitting back in my chair studying me very closely. On the other hand, I wondered, had she been studying my reaction to her revelations. I had no idea what kind of thoughts go on in a child's mind.

One thing I will admit too is an annoyance. Look, this might sound selfish but I was the number one session artist (or stand-in in singer) with the group and had been for some years by then. To have Jan stroll in and take over as lead singer ... well, that old snake jealousy began to raise its ugly head. Only I can't explain why, all I did was sing a few songs with boys, now and again.

Mind you, they had been on at me for years to become a permanent member of the group.

Feeling uncomfortable under Chrissie's insistent gaze, I suggested that we went round to the garage so I could say hello to her mother.

Janet Symonds and all of the guys had their backs to us as we entered the garage. They were halfway through a rendition of Dolly Parton's "I Want to Hold You In My Dreams Tonight!" and making a damned good job of the number until Mike brought in to a halt to suggest the two guys adding harmonies did something a little differently. Then they re-started a few bars before they broke off.

All the members of the group were so into what they were doing that none of them was aware that Chrissie and I had entered the garage. Not wishing to disturb them, we went around behind the Rolls and I hoisted the child up so she could sit on the workbench, then I sat myself beside her and we observed the rehearsal from there.

What surprised me more than anything was the fact that Jan appeared to know exactly what she was doing. Look, singing and performing for the public ain't quite the same thing. Watching Jan … or should I say Janet Symonds rehearsing, assured me that I was looking at a performer, not any old singer. Had she got into the scene a lot younger, before she'd married that clown Andrew, I figured Janet Symonds could have been a star performer.

I had to admit that Janet could bash out those Country Ballads when she chose to. Chrissie and I must have sat there for a couple of hours almost transfixed. That is until one guys spotted us … or should that be me, sitting there watching, and very unsubtly picked-out the start of the Chords of 'Proud Mary' on his guitar.

Mike and Jan instantly spun around looking for me.

I should make it clear that the guys in the group had had carte blanche to rehearse in my garage for some years by then. It was a particularly large three-bayed building, which had once been the coach house for the much larger country house that had originally stood on the site.

Mike had a key and the band would come and go as they wished, and often did without me being at the property. When they were there, I found them; they didn't even come and disturb me from my work.

A big smile came on Jan's face when she saw Chrissie sitting there beside me. Jan was still very conscious of the animosity the child had originally displayed towards me. I'm not too sure that the two females talked ... or rather confided in each other as much as mothers and daughters are supposed to do. Maybe that had been the reason Chrissie had been such a daddies' girl in the first place.

"Well, what do you think?" Jan asked, quite obviously talking about her performance.

While my nose had been put out of joint ... more than a little, I still had to admit to her that Janet Symonds was going to wow them at the Ponderosa. And any other

C&W venue they were booked to perform at. So I told her as much. I gave her a long and flattering speech about how brilliant a performer she was and suggested that I thought her contribution to the band ... group or whatever you want to call it, would take them all too new heights.

No, I didn't mention or show that I was pissed-off that Jan was about to usurp any position I held with the band and/or its fans.

Jan did ask me if we could rehearse a few duets together, but I explained that I had a deadline to meet and had to get back to the grindstone. Of course, there was no deadline, just a very pissed-off Tug Wilson, who was quite definitely sulking.

The old line "No good deed goes unpunished!" crept into my mind and I vowed never to involve myself in other people's troubles in the future.

I rarely went near the Ponderosa on live music nights during the winter months anyway. Because the bar wasn't all that large and when packed with revellers, it was almost impossible to move, let alone breathe. However, I was made aware that the group's new lead singer was a great hit with the public. Bert even had a big sign made to put out by the road, announcing that Janet Symonds was appearing there that evening.

I did not see Jan round the town either and her presence in the office there even brought my 'drop in for coffee' visits to Pete's garage to an end. I even released the tiebacks on the net curtains of my study, so that Chrissie, James and Vicky couldn't see if I was in there when they accompanied Jan to the group's rehearsals.

When the Rolls or Land Rover needed a service, I asked Pete to collect and deliver them back again, arranging, when I could, that he did so while I was away visiting my sister Jean. Pete knew me too well and I was aware that he'd ask me some difficult to answer questions about why I hadn't been near the garage of late. And why I was avoiding Jan and the children.

I couldn't think of any valid reason why I was avoiding everyone. Jan didn't need me anymore. I had got the basic scenario for a novel if I ever decided to write it.

I just felt uncomfortable to be around Jan and the kids, after all, we'd always hated each other, or was I just gun shy after the betrayal of Laura.

But why couldn't I get Jan out of my thoughts if I couldn't stand the woman? Try as I might I just couldn't seem to concentrate on my writing, she was always creeping into my thoughts.

THE CENOTAPH

It was mid-October and several months since I'd seen Pete or spoken to Jan.

 I had just climbed out of bed and made it to the kitchen. When I heard the front door opening. Then a loud voice shouting "Morning Cockwoble rise and shine" "Bugger off Pete I'm in the kitchen" I filled the kettle and put it on to boil. Pete wandered in and sat at the kitchen table. "What's up with you lately Tug. Are you avoiding us we've not seen you down the garage for ages."

"Naw, just have been busy deadlines to meet. Anyway, what are you doing here at silly o'clock in the morning"

"Got an invite yesterday through the post from Major Jennings to attend the Cenotaph Parade on the 11th November. Then got a phone call last night from him. You, and me my old mucker are under orders. The old man said I was to make sure that Sergeant Raymond Wilson was there with the medal, or he would have us both recalled and scrubbing out all the shithouses in Lympstone with a toothbrush."

"Bugger that Pete you know that every year on the 11th I disappear on Bonnie. I don't need reminding of that nightmare. I still wake up in the middle of the night in a cold sweat seeing Geordie with no head. Plus the leg still gives me Gip on cold mornings"

"Now you listen to me Tug, you're not the only one who has those flashbacks and nightmares from that day. Geordie was my mate as well. So stop feeling sorry for yourself and get your head out of your arse. Yes, I know you had it rough what with Laura buggering off with that wanker while you were in the hospital. That's life, mate, life goes on. Now whether you like it or not you're coming up to town on the 10th. We have rooms booked at the Victory Club. Then on the 11th, we will parade with the lads and do the march past. You will wear that medal. You'll wear it for Geordie and the lads who never made it back. Am I making myself clear Sergeant Wilson?"

"Ok, Pete I suppose I don't have much choice when you put it like that"

"And you will wear the medal. A lot of the lads wouldn't have made it if you hadn't thrown a wobbly and taken out those Argies. Wear the medal with pride it's for all the lads. Besides, we don't want those wankers from the Paras to show us up. Then it's a massive piss up after the parade."

11th November found us all milling about at the start of the parade. I was looking about recognising many familiar faces all proudly wearing their coveted Green Lids (Berets) and displaying their hard-earned medals on their breasts.

Major Jennings came up to me and Pete, warmly greeting us and shaking our hands.

Then he looked at his watch and gave the order "SERGEANT WILSON TAKE CHARGE GET THE MEN FELL IN"

In a voice I had not used for 10 years, I shouted the order.

"PARADE...PARADE, FALL IN....... DRESS RANKS..... RIGHT TURN" then as the parade moved off "BY THE LEFT QUICK MARCH" We marched down the Mall past the Cenotaph Major Jennings in the lead myself just behind him Pete was marching to my left out of the corner of my eye I could have sworn I could see Geordie marching alongside.

After the parade was, dismissed. Things became a bit hazy after the beer began flowing. The usual insults were good-naturedly exchanged between the Paras and Marines.

After arriving home I decided I must be getting old it took at least 3 days before I started feeling anywhere near human again.

I was still avoiding the garage and Jan. I was concentrating on trying to find some inspiration for my writing. I decided I needed a break and change of scenery. I was stuck in a writer's block, I needed fresh inspiration.

In the early part of December, I upset Jean by announcing that I was off to spend Christmas in southern Italy. It wasn't unknown for me to spend some of the winter months in southern Europe somewhere. My profession made it convenient for temporary relocation during the colder winter months. It helped research new locations to set stories in. It also made it easier on my old war wound. However, my sister liked me to visit with her and her family over the holiday.

I loaded all my junk in the back of the Rolla and set off to catch the ferry at Dover. Yeah I could have used the tunnel but I enjoy the short boat trip more, and it kind-a confirmed that you are going abroad, you could say. I had no idea where I was going, but had a vague idea about heading for Rome and possibly Naples for starters; then on down further where I could look-up a couple of old friends I hadn't seen for a good few years or so.

Because I was so uncommitted or you could say, unconfined as far as my itinerary went, and my sat-nav was telling me that I'd be passing near to Nancy, I decided that I'd stop-off there and visit an old mate (read drinking buddy) from my Royal Marine days. French people hadn't been high on my favoured people list until I'd served with Jack. (His dad was French and his mum was English) Okay, Jacques but he had always been Jack to me. We ... err, well, for a Frenchman he could put the beer away. Mind Laura wasn't too enamoured that he went after all her mates, but that's Frenchmen for you; frustrated Casanova's all of the buggers.

Whatever I'd run into Jack at Heathrow a couple of years previous; we'd only had a couple of minutes to talk, because his flight had been called, but he had given me his address in France and insisted that I should call-in, if and when I was passing. Several times, I'd driven to the south of France and Italy during the intervening years but neglected to stop-by; just bad planning and/or lack of time I think. This time I vowed to go out of my way to call in to visit Jack and his family.

It was quite late in the day before I tracked Jacque's house down, a few kilometres west of Nancy. It was a small and somewhat dilapidated looking establishment tucked away on a minor road. But like many small French farms, looks can be deceiving. I have no idea who the young woman who opened to the door was. I was sure that she wasn't Jacque's daughter anyway, because she informed me -- rather brusquely -- that the "Madame and Monsieur would return shortly!" and she didn't invite me inside to wait for them.

Strangely, that was to prove advantageous for me, because my original idea had been to stay-over for a few days, had Jacques and his wife invited me. However, after I'd waited half an hour Jacques and his wife did return. Then -- much to my surprise -- Sandra

(Laura's bosom buddy at university and the chief bridesmaid at our wedding) climbed out of the passenger seat of Jacque's Renault.

Shall we say, it was an uncomfortable and somewhat awkward reunion? Jacques did invite me to stopover, but I suddenly remembered an appointment that required my presence in Berne first thing the following morning.

I believe I was attempting to make it to Rome before I stopped again for a proper rest. But I ended up stopping at a small off the beaten track Pensione somewhere after Milan, but before I passed Bologna. No, I don't know for sure, some local police or Carabineer officer anyway, gave me directions to it. I was pretty well knackered by then. It was in a nice quiet area though, so I spent a couple of days there wandering around the countryside hoping I'd feel inspired to write something. I didn't!

So after three or it might have been as many as five nights with the weather not being too clever, I moved further south to Rome, but changed my mind because the "Been there done Rome!" atmosphere began to pervade my vehicle as I started to battle my way through the traffic to get into the city.

Italian drivers become a law unto themselves, especially when driving in a city. The more of them there are, trying to use a specific piece of tarmac, the more chaos seems to ensue.

Mind you, Naples wasn't much better, but nothing will ever tire me of being around Pompeii and/or Herculaneum. I wandered around both sets ruins for days-on-end trying to think of something to write. Maybe even something serious, instead of the tripe I was in the habit of churning out. I was inspired to a point, but it was only the outline for a couple of ... banal romances and I only managed a couple of thousand words of those. I couldn't get my teeth into either story.

So I moved even further south to call-in on a couple of acquaintances, mostly ex-pats who had emigrated to warmer climes many years before. I always found it too damned hot down there during the summer months.

I spent Christmas with an artist friend, his wife and his model, who I do believe was not only his mistress but also his wife's lover. A very strange household, but also an interesting one. Another outline got typed into the computer, but that was as far as anything got.

I travelled quiet roads and hills on foot, toured ruins and churches, and spent too many hours sitting in and outside bars watching Italian women walk by. And of course, I drank too much Italian beer, damned stuff never agrees with me. I'll add that even the Italian females that I did see, failed to inspire me to write anything.

That's roughly how the next few months went. I travelled up the Adriatic coast of Italy, then cut across the country into France, before I got up as far as Venice. Laura and I had honeymooned in that city, so I've tended to avoid the place ever since.

Whatever, as the days and weeks passed I travelled along the Mediterranean coast into Spain and down to Gibraltar. Stopping here and there for a few days at a time, mostly in Pensioners and small hotels off the beaten tourist track.

Was I inspired to write anything? Well, yes I did come up with a few outlines and/or scenarios. But could I get my mind into writing mode? No, I bloody-well couldn't and I had no idea why."

I might have started out driving the Rolls down to Naples, but I ended-up almost three months later in Gibraltar. I just couldn't settle anywhere for more than a day or two and I was suffering from my worst attack of writer's block ever.

"Jesus H Christ, who's died?" Yvonne's familiar voice suddenly woke me from my mussing.

I was sat outside a bar not far from a quay in Gib, nursing a half-empty glass of British beer. I do not know where my mind had been, before Yvonne's voice broke through the haze.

"Bugger Yvonne, where did you spring from? What are you doing here?" I asked.

"Taking a short break away from the grindstone. I was going to ask you what you are doing here, Tug. The last I heard you were in Italy. Did you take a wrong turn somewhere?"

"Not exactly, I just can't seem to find the right ambience to write in. I've been wandering all over bloody Europe like a lost sheep."

"Lack of the right ambience, are you sure that's your problem, Tug?"

"Well, what else could it be?"

"How about the lack of the right company?"

"Oh don't talk nonsense, Yvonne; I write alone, you know that."

"Yes you do write alone, Tug, but you're usually surrounded by your friends; well a few close friends anyway."

"Yvonne, I don't do friends, you know that. I have a few business acquaintances, like yourself and even less family, that's all."

"That's odd because I happen to know one particular friend, and her children, who are wondering where their White Knight has disappeared to?"

I have no idea what kind of expression those words from Yvonne brought to my face, but she went on.

"Janet is divorced now, Tug. She's a free agent and she's very upset that someone has vanished from her life. So are her children; what did you do to those two youngsters? They keep calling my office asking my people if they know when you are coming back to the UK."

"Look, Yvonne, Jan an' me ... well, we're never really friends. Okay, we went to school together, but we hated each others' guts all the time we were at school. Nothing has changed, except that when we met again we ... well, we were more adult about it!"

"And Janet needed help with her divorce?"

"Yes."

"And out of the kindness of his heart, soft old Tug Wilson came to her aid."

"Yes, that's all there was to it!"

"Oh, that's bloody awkward. Because while he was playing the White Knight, Janet Symonds saw through the bad boy image Tug likes to portray to the world and fell in love with the man inside."

"Rubbish Yvonne, she's on the rebound."

"I don't believe so, Tug. She might have been mixed-up once, but Janet has her head screwed on the right way round now; that's one thing I am sure of! And what's more, she tells me that she's in love with you, even though you can be an arrogant bastard, when you choose to be. Jan's description, not mine by the way."

Yvonne smiled at me and took her mobile phone out of her handbag.

"Want me to prove it, Tug? All I've got to do is call Janet and I'll bet you she'll be on the next flight out here. She's already been to Italy twice looking for you."

"Oh Christ, what do I do now?" I asked.

"Your choice handsome. I can make the call, or you can get in that Rolls Royce parked outside the Holiday Inn hotel and get you backside back to the UK a bit sharpish. That woman needs a caring man in her life. Mind you, so do those Children. You wouldn't believe it, from the stink he kicked-up about custody, but that father of theirs hasn't been near the children since the divorce was finalised."

The Rolla was an absolute tip inside by the time I drove off the ferry in Dover. I'd slept in the thing, not stopping long enough anywhere to take a hotel room and I needed a bath something rotten. However, I still didn't stop and drove directly to Jan's house, parking on the drive beside her Disco at some unearthly hour of the morning. I must have been tired and have gone out like a light.

When I awoke again, Chrissie's face was staring back at me through the side window ... smiling. I could see James milling around behind her, apparently doing battle with a tangled vacuum cleaner cable and hose. The water drops on the windows informed me that the Rolls had been washed on the outside while I slept inside it.

I hit the button that lowered the window.

"Coffee's hot, but mummy's in the kitchen with it, waiting for you. I think you might be in big trouble, Uncle Tug!" Chrissie grinned at me.

It took a couple of years but I've become dad not to both James and Chrissie now. I'm not their biological father, but I appear to be a much-loved stepfather.

Chrissie got her swing in the tree just after all three of them moved in with me. And that was before Jan and I took our vows, I have to admit.

Do Jan and I disagree? Sure we do. We never can agree on the order of songs in the next set. And of course, is it "Tug and Janet Symonds-Wilson", or "Janet Symonds-Wilson and Tug Wilson" on the billboards. But rarely do we disagree on the important things in life like ... shall we go to bed now?

Oh yeah, and I did give Mr Andrew Halfon a smack on the nose; more than one smack, to be precise. He turned up unexpectedly as we were packing up after a gig one night; he left again in an ambulance. However, he did take a swing at me first, so I was simply defending myself, wasn't I? No, I never pressed charges. Well, after all, I'd won the prize, hadn't I?

Life goes on

Printed in Great Britain
by Amazon

44424843R00132

More Cozy Mysteries by Cindy Bell

Heavenly Highland Inn Cozy Mystery Series

Murdering the Roses

Dead in the Daisies

Killing the Carnations

Drowning the Daffodils

Bekki the Beautician Cozy Mystery Series

Hairspray and Homicide

A Dyed Blonde and a Dead Body

Mascara and Murder

Pageant and Poison

Conditioner and a Corpse

Makeup, Mistletoe and Murder

Hairpin, Hair Dryer and Homicide

Blush, a Bride and Body

Shampoo and a Stiff

Table of Contents

Chapter One... 1

Chapter Two 15

Chapter Three...46

Chapter Four... 67

Chapter Five 86

Chapter Six 97

Chapter Seven...116

Chapter Eight... 139

Chapter One

The dew covered leaves on the bushes glistened in the sun as the gardener leaned closer to a bright yellow blossom that had bloomed overnight.

"Have you ever seen anything so exquisite?" he asked with admiration. Vicky smiled at the man. She loved to see anyone with passion for their work, and felt very lucky that he had recently started working at the Heavenly Highland Inn. She and her older sister, Sarah, had the same passion for the beautiful, old inn that they had inherited after their parents passed. At first it had been an adjustment for Vicky to settle into a life as the Events Director of the inn, she was used to roaming as she pleased. But ever since she and her sister had taken over the day to day running of the inn, Vicky had found a passion for their childhood home, and the happiness it brought to those who visited it. She considered it her responsibility to create lasting and treasured memories for their guests, as special and beautiful as the blossom that the gardener was admiring.

"It is stunning," Vicky agreed as she leaned down to take a proper look at the flower. Just as she was standing back up, the peaceful morning was ripped to shreds by the sound of an obnoxiously loud motorcycle. Vicky narrowed her eyes and turned in the direction of the large, sweeping driveway that sloped uphill. She watched as a big, black motorcycle with bright green accents roared right up to the front of the inn. Vicky was suspicious as she watched. Most of their guests tended to be the very wealthy and the elite of not just the country, but the world. Despite the fact that their inn was in a small town that most people had never heard of, it had an amazing reputation for luxury, privacy, and of course, excellent parties and events. So, to see a motorcycle pull up was quite unusual.

Vicky continued to observe as the driver of the motorcycle climbed off. The person had a very slight frame and Vicky guessed that it was a woman, but she couldn't tell too much because of the big, black helmet that covered her head, the black leather jacket she wore, the matching black leather pants, and the high, black boots that finished off the outfit. As the figure walked towards her, Vicky began to grow a little more anxious. She glanced over at the gardener who seemed to be just as confused as she was.

"Can I help you?" she asked in a stern voice as the person completely covered in black paused before her. She even had gloves covering her hands, which raised to the sides of her helmet and tugged it upward. Vicky gasped when her Aunt Ida's face was revealed. Her Aunt Ida had lived at the inn for as long as she could remember. After Vicky's parents died she became a very important part of her life, as well as her sister's. But Aunt Ida, despite being advanced in age, was not one to sit back and knit or watch re-runs. She was the most vivacious and exhausting person that Vicky knew, and she never failed to come up with a new way to surprise her nieces, including the fact that she had dyed her hair black, and caked her lips with a red lipstick so bright that Vicky suspected it might have been some kind of paint instead of make-up.

"Aunt Ida?" she asked with wide eyes and a slow shake of her head. "What are you up to, now?"

"That's what I'd like to know," Sarah said as she stepped out of the front door of the inn. Vicky assumed she had come to find out what all the noise had been. The gardener took his cue to leave as the three women who ran the inn together stood beside each other. Sarah narrowed her eyes and crossed her arms. Vicky tried not to laugh as Aunt Ida unzipped her leather jacket to reveal a skin-tight, black t-shirt with a skull and crossbones on the front.

Although, Vicky and Sarah knew Aunt Ida's true age, at least they thought they did, Aunt Ida could easily pass for being in her forties. She was a gorgeous woman with or without make-up, and she had a figure that no amount of dieting, exercising or body-shaping had ever been able to give Vicky. She easily gained the attention of many of their male guests, but she was not one to dwell on one man for very long.

"Aunt Ida, please don't tell me that thing belongs to you," Sarah said crossly as she studied her aunt. Sarah was a few years older than Vicky, but they couldn't have more different lives. Sarah was married to a wonderful man, and had children of her own. She lived in a house nearby, and always put her family first in every decision she made, especially when it came to taking risks. Vicky on the other hand took after her Aunt Ida, she had her independent spirit and preferred to explore the world, and live each moment to the fullest. She was currently in her longest-lasting relationship, with to everyone's surprise, a newly appointed detective within the local police department.

"Of course it's mine, didn't you see the plate?" Aunt Ida asked and pointed out the vanity plate on the back of the motorcycle. It said 'Ida's Ride'.

"Oh my," Sarah sighed and shook her head. "Don't you realize how dangerous motorcycles are?" she asked.

"Dangerous if you don't know what you're doing," Aunt Ida agreed. "I took a class!"

"Just one class?" Vicky asked nervously as she studied her aunt. She was a slender woman, but she had no problem taking care of herself. She had a black belt and knew exactly how to use it. However, a black belt wouldn't protect her from road rash.

"No, not just one," Ida replied with a gleam in her eyes. "Actually, it was several classes, and a few dinners," she wiggled her eyebrows.

"Oh, Aunt Ida," Sarah sighed heavily.

"What's a couple of meals between friends?" Ida giggled.

"Oh, Aunt Ida," Vicky laughed and rolled her eyes. "You're always getting into something."

"Something amazing," Aunt Ida corrected. "I opened this baby up on a back country road, and it felt like I was flying!"

"You weren't speeding, were you?" Sarah demanded impatiently. "Don't you realize what could happen if you got into an accident?"

"I'm not going to get into an accident," Aunt Ida pursed her red lips, she always had the attitude that life was worth living and not to limit your enjoyment of it because of something that might never happen. "Unfortunately, we know that accidents can happen even if you are very cautious and doing everything right," Aunt Ida said, referring to the tragic accident that had killed the sisters' parents. "I will never overstep the mark and risk my life or anyone else's."

"I know, but..." Sarah started to say.

"Listen, you two wet blankets, you're not going to ruin my fun. Now, if either of you want a ride, you just let me know, otherwise, you keep your noses out of it!"

Vicky had to suppress another laugh as she always found it amusing when her aunt was angry. She was very dramatic when she was offended.

"We will," Vicky promised, though Sarah didn't look as convinced. "But, just remember, no speeding."

"Yeah, yeah," Ida waved her hand and walked away on her tall, black boots.

"Do you think she's getting a little senile?" Sarah asked as she stepped closer to her sister.

"Not at all," Vicky laughed and shook her head. "Aunt Ida just likes to try new things."

"I guess, but doesn't it worry you? Motorcycles are not safe!" Sarah said with conviction.

"Well, I think Aunt Ida can make her own choices," Vicky said confidently. "I'm sure she'll be as cautious as she needs to be."

"Aunt Ida? Cautious?" Sarah shook her head and walked away. Vicky turned back to take one last look at the beautiful garden. She had no idea what the day had in store for her, but she was certain that it was going to be interesting.

***

Not long after Aunt Ida roared off on her motorcycle, another vehicle that commanded Vicky's attention just as much pulled into the driveway of the inn. It was a shiny Aston Martin, one of the most expensive cars in existence. Although, the inn normally catered to wealthy clients, this car was one that Vicky had never laid eyes on in person before. She wasn't impressed very much by expensive things, but she had to admit, that the sleek, silver car was beautiful.

Vicky walked towards it as a couple stepped out of the car. The man appeared to be in his early forties with his sandy, blonde hair thinning slightly on top. He wore reflective sunglasses, and a tailored suit. The woman who paused beside him was statuesque in height, having at least two inches on the man who Vicky assumed was her husband. She had deeply tanned skin, and her hair was a mixture of light brown and chocolate brown. She wore a simple pants suit that was accentuated by exquisite crystal jewelry. Her almond shaped eyes were a deep brown shade that seemed more open and accepting than critical, until they swung towards her husband.

"Are you going to get the bags?" she asked him impatiently.

"I'm sure they have someone to do that," he replied dismissively and reached up to take off his sunglasses. It was in that moment that Vicky recognized him. She had seen him on the cover of a magazine. He was considered one of the countries luckiest men because he had married into one of the richest families in the United States. The Lambards owned many businesses including the most recent and the most profitable addition, a steel manufacturing plant.

The addition of the plant had made the family even wealthier. Now, the heiress to the Lambard family fortune, Sandy Holstead, was standing in front of the inn looking around expectantly. Vicky wasn't aware of any high profile clients arriving so early in the day, and she assumed that her sister wasn't aware of their arrival either. She hurried across the parking lot towards the Holsteads and attempted to portray the same professional image her sister would.

"Hello," she greeted them both with a warm smile. "I'm Vicky, and I'm one of the owners of the Heavenly Highland Inn," she explained as they both turned to look at her. "I can get your bags, if you'd like."

"Wonderful," Mr. Holstead said and dropped the keys to the car into Vicky's outstretched palm. "They're in the trunk, but please do be careful not to tear the upholstery or scuff the trunk when you take the bags out," he spoke very carefully to her, as if he were explaining something to a child. Vicky tightened her lips a little, but only nodded respectfully.

"Oh, Gerald, relax, it's just a car not a piece of art," Sandy said dismissively and smiled apologetically at Vicky.

"See, that's the problem," Gerald huffed as he turned to face his wife, his annoyance clear in the crease of his brow. "Just because it's not hanging on a museum wall somewhere doesn't mean that it's not art, Sandy. This car is priceless, and perfect, and I want to keep it that way."

"Well, it certainly did have a price," Sandy replied in an abrasive tone. "A very large and ridiculous price as I recall."

"Here we go again," Gerald sighed and hung his head in defeat. "I thought this weekend was supposed to be about us calling a truce?" he asked as he met his wife's eyes. Vicky couldn't help but overhear the spat as she pulled the luggage out of the trunk of the car. It surprised her that people with so much money could still have so much difficulty in life. But then, money doesn't create happiness, Vicky had seen that with the guests at the inn often enough to believe in that saying. As she hauled the large suitcases up to the porch Sarah walked out of the front door.

"Oh, are the Holsteads here already?" she asked with surprise. "They weren't supposed to arrive until this evening."

"Trust me, you don't want to cause any more friction between those two," Vicky warned as she hobbled past her sister with the bags. "Just find them a room away from other guests, because I don't think they're going to make it through the night without an explosive argument."

"Thanks for the warning," Sarah murmured before she walked out to greet the Holsteads.

Vicky placed the bags on a luggage cart. Then she charged a concierge with their care. As she walked back towards the kitchen to check on the meal preparation for lunch, she could hear the Holsteads squabbling over whether they wanted a room that overlooked the gardens or the pool.

Chapter Two

When Vicky stepped into the kitchen she found Chef Henry dancing around the large island in the middle of it. He had some lively music playing and seemed to be very involved in preparing the last of the breakfast meals as he dashed them with salt and pepper to the beat of the music. Vicky suppressed a giggle and decided not to interrupt him, but before she could back away and slip through the door, Sarah stepped in behind her.

"Wow, he's really got some moves," Sarah said with appreciation and a laugh as she nudged Vicky with her elbow.

"Oh!" Henry stopped in the middle of a spin to find both sisters staring at him. "How long have you been watching?" he asked with a cluck of his tongue, and narrowed eyes.

"Long enough to know that you're dancing with me at the next wedding we put on," Vicky said with a determined grin dancing across her lips.

"And what would Mitchell think?" Sarah asked reproachfully though her eyes were shining with mirth.

"He'd probably feel relieved that he wouldn't end up with bruises on his feet," Vicky laughed and shook her head. "I'm not exactly the most graceful person on the dance floor," she added in a whisper, as if it was a confession.

"Oh honey, I could change that," Henry said with a light wink as a waitress came to take the breakfast plates to the dining room. "Now, what can I do for you two?"

Sarah set her lips into a grim line and Vicky could tell from her straightened posture that she had just shifted into business mode.

"I need you to do me a favor and gather all of the products that contain peanuts in the kitchen. I need you to make sure the kitchen is wiped down and all the utensils and dishes are cleaned," Sarah said firmly.

"Why?" Vicky asked with confusion as Henry nodded in response to Sarah's requests and began to gather a few items off the counter.

"Sandy Holstead is allergic to peanuts," Sarah explained as she glanced over at Vicky. "If she's exposed to it she has such a severe allergic reaction that she could die."

"Oh, I didn't know that," Henry exclaimed.

"I'm sorry to spring this on you so suddenly," Sarah added with a frown. "I thought we'd have until this evening to prepare, but they arrived early."

"It's no problem," Henry assured her.

"Oh, it must be hard to go through life with such a terrible allergy," Vicky said with a frown. "Yes, we had better make sure everything in the inn is safe."

"I am," Sarah assured her. "I asked Sandy and Gerald to wait out by the pool while I made sure their room was deep cleaned. I just hope she doesn't end up pushing him in," she added with widened eyes.

"Well, maybe it would cool off their bickering," Vicky giggled and ducked when Sarah took a swipe at her with her palm. "Kidding!" Vicky promised, but Sarah set her jaw.

"It is very important that everything goes to plan during their stay, they could be a great source of high-end referrals for us," she explained.

"We can store the non-perishables out in the shed," Henry suggested as he grabbed a box from the supply closet. He began boxing up items immediately. Vicky was about to ask Sarah if she knew how the Holsteads had come to book a weekend at their relatively small resort. It was luxurious of course, but the Holsteads could afford to go to other countries, or even to rent their own island so, as always, she was interested to know why they had chosen their inn. It was always useful to have this information as it often helped with marketing. Before she could ask, her cell phone began to ring. She checked the caller ID and found that it was Mitchell. She answered right away with a smile.

"Hey stranger," she said with a playful southern drawl.

"Who are you and what have you done with my Vicky?" Mitchell demanded in a playful response.

"Ha ha," Vicky laughed into the phone. "You would not believe what I just saw!" she said with excitement.

"What?" he asked with interest building.

"A real Aston Martin, in person!" she squealed into the phone as she stepped out of the kitchen.

"At a car show?" Mitchell asked with disbelief.

"No, at the inn," she laughed as she walked down the hall. "The Holsteads are staying at the inn."

"Oh, wow," Mitchell said, genuinely impressed. "You must have your hands full."

"Not really," she said quickly. "Sarah's handling most of it. I was hoping you might be able to meet me for dinner tonight. I know it's short notice," she added. She and Mitchell hadn't seen each other much lately though they had talked on the phone every day.

"I wish I could," Mitchell sighed with disappointment. "You have no idea how much I want to," she could hear him frowning over the phone and the longing in his tone.

"Are you working late again?" Vicky asked with dismay. "You've been working late every night for over a week!"

"Yes, Sheriff McDonald is still angry with me. I questioned him on one of the cases we were investigating, so he has me pulling double shifts," he groaned. "I can't say that I regret speaking up, but he sure is making me pay for it."

"That man," Vicky said with annoyance but stopped herself before saying too much. She didn't like the way that Sheriff McDonald treated

Mitchell, but she also knew how important Mitchell's job was to him.

"I know, I know," he sighed again. "But it can't go on forever."

"I hope not," Vicky replied with a hint of a pout in her voice. "I miss you."

"I miss you, too, Vicky," he replied in a loving tone. "Don't worry, he has to let me sleep sometime."

That's what you think, Vicky thought to herself. She suspected that Sheriff McDonald was trying to see how long it would take for Mitchell to break. She also knew that Sheriff McDonald would have a very long wait. Mitchell was one of the most patient and determined people that she had ever known.

"You're not upset are you?" Mitchell asked cautiously.

"No, I'm not," Vicky said quickly. "I understand, I do actually have a bridal shower to plan anyway," she added as she reached her apartment, which consisted of several rooms that had been converted into an apartment for her to live in so that there would always be someone in charge living in the inn. Aunt Ida also lived in one of the guest rooms at the inn but she was not really active in running the inn, she was more active in getting into trouble.

"Thanks for understanding," Mitchell said. "I'll see you soon, I promise."

"I'm always here," Vicky pointed out with a laugh before she hung up the phone. She settled down at her work desk in her office and opened up the plans she had been working on for the bridal shower. They were doing it for free for a waitress that worked in one of the restaurants in town. It was a way to generate good word of mouth advertising, and to give back to the community. Vicky was very excited about it because she was going to plan it from beginning to end. Usually she had to make choices based on the input or desires of the client. In this case she was getting to choose almost all of the elements of the bridal shower, which she really enjoyed.

Vicky was looking over some color schemes when she heard loud voices coming from the pool area. Her apartment was only a short distance from the pool. She couldn't quite make out what the voices were saying, but she could tell that they were angry. She waited a few moments, hoping that the argument would calm down. She assumed it was Sandy and Gerald fighting. When the voices rose even louder instead of calming, Vicky stood up from her desk. Although the Holsteads were important guests she had to think of the comfort of the other guests that were staying in the inn. No one went on a weekend vacation to hear someone arguing. Vicky walked down the walkway to the pool area. She could hear snippets of their conversation as she did.

"Look at this pool," Sandy was insisting. "It's beautiful and clear, it doesn't even smell of chlorine like most of the pools we swim in do. I want to spend the day swimming and tanning tomorrow."

"We came here to relax," Gerald argued in return. "What could be more relaxing than the spa and massage package?"

"I don't want that, I can have that any place we go. This pool won't be anywhere else we go," she pointed out with determination.

"This weekend was supposed to be for us," Gerald responded heatedly.

"I'm not the one who chose this place," Sandy shot back. "This inn I've never heard of in the middle of nowhere, you were the one who insisted we come here. So, we're going to do what I want to do," she added, her voice raising with every word she spoke. There was so much tension between the couple that by the time Vicky walked up to them, she expected either one to launch a physical attack at any moment. She knew that she needed to say something to break the tension.

"Excuse me," she said with a warm smile as she stepped through the gate that led to the pool. "I just wanted to check if you would like to have lunch at the inn? We have a private room that I can reserve for you if you'd rather dine by yourselves, or if you would prefer you can have it in the main dining room."

Both of the Holsteads turned to look at Vicky with abrupt disdain at having their argument interrupted.

"No, we'll just have room service," Gerald snapped.

"Yes, it would probably be best if we stayed holed up in our room," Sandy sighed and shook her head with defeat. "No one wants to hear us argue over soup or salad."

Vicky smiled compassionately.

"I'm sure your room is just about ready, and if there's anything either of you need, please feel free to ask," she added and looked from one to the other. She hoped they would be able to find some kind of peace or relaxation during their weekend at the inn. Most people were swept into a bit of a fantasy life when they stayed at the Heavenly Highland Inn, but it seemed as if these two were going to need something that had a much bigger impact than a weekend at the inn. Though she and Mitchell had their share of disagreements they rarely argued. Then again, they weren't married, or even living together. Vicky imagined that changed the level of arguing in a relationship. Just then one of the maids arrived to walk Sandy and Gerald to their room.

"Actually, there is one thing I would like," Sandy said as Gerald began to follow the maid. "I would love a glass of wine," she smiled at Vicky.

"A glass of wine? You can't wait until lunch?" Gerald demanded with frustration. "Are you planning to be sloshed by dessert?"

"Save it, Gerald," Sandy rolled her eyes and settled back down at the table. "If I want a glass of wine by the pool, I'm going to have it. In case you were wondering, you're not invited," she added with a flash in her eyes. Gerald's cheeks grew red with anger and Vicky averted her gaze respectfully from the squabble. She wasn't sure what to say to alleviate the tension.

"We have a nice chardonnay," she murmured as she glanced at Sandy.

"That sounds perfect," Sandy agreed with a nod. She seemed entirely undisturbed by her husband's fury as he stalked off after the maid. Vicky was relieved to walk away as well. She headed for the kitchen to make sure that Chef Henry knew that the Holsteads wanted room service and to get Sandy her glass of wine. Vicky walked into the kitchen to find a relatively new sous chef preparing the salads that would accompany the main dish of the lunch that was being served.

"Hello, Peter," Vicky said with a small smile as she met the eyes of the man before her. He was young, maybe in his early twenties. He was new to town and Henry had taken a chance on him because he liked to provide work for the locals.

"Yes, ma'am," Peter said and lowered his eyes. He seemed fairly shy, which Vicky found to be endearing.

"Where's Chef Henry?" she asked as she glanced around the kitchen.

"He is talking with a few of the guests in the dining room," Peter replied as he finished the last salad.

"Well, can you please inform him that the Holsteads would like their lunch in their room?" Vicky asked politely.

"Oh, I can take it up to them," Peter offered with a shrug.

"No," Vicky said firmly. "I'd prefer it if it was Chef Henry who took them their food, okay?" she raised an eyebrow and waited for Peter to look up at her. He had pale blue eyes that seemed as evasive as his demeanor.

"Sure, of course," he nodded.

"Could you get me a glass of chardonnay for Mrs. Holstead?" she inquired. "Better make it a large one," she added as an afterthought. She was sure that Sandy was going to need something to relax her.

"Absolutely," he nodded and retrieved one of the glasses. He opened a new bottle of wine and poured the drink into the glass, then handed it to Vicky.

"Thanks," she replied. As she took the glass from him she thought she had better be sure that he knew about Sandy's allergy. "Did Chef Henry tell you to make sure there are no products with peanuts in the kitchen?" Vicky asked.

"Yes, don't worry, everything with peanuts is out," he assured her. Vicky nodded and then she carried the glass out to Sandy who was staring out across the grounds. The view from the pool was idyllic as it was of the blooming gardens set against a backdrop of rolling hills that blended into the thick woods.

"Here you are, Mrs. Holstead," Vicky said as she walked up to her.

"Thank you, so much," Sandy replied as she accepted the glass of wine. "Please, will you sit with me for a moment?" she suggested. "I do hate to drink alone, but my husband is not very good company at the moment."

Vicky sat down at the table beside her and spoke carefully, she didn't want to appear as if she was prying.

"He seems a bit out of sorts," she offered.

"A bit?" Sandy laughed at that and took a big swallow of her wine. For the first time Vicky suspected that this wasn't the only wine she'd had so far that day. "Oh, Gerald is never happy," she sighed and swirled her wine in the glass. "The truth is, that my husband's eyes have been wandering," Sandy slurred as she drank a gulp of her wine. She leaned back in her chair and gazed out over the sky. "I'm not bad to look at, am I?" she asked as she glanced over at Vicky.

"Not at all," Vicky replied as she smiled sympathetically at the woman. "You're very beautiful."

"And rich," Sandy added as she took another large sip of her wine. "You might think that would be enough to keep a man happy. But, no, not Gerald," she sighed, her shoulders drooped, and her eyes nearly fell shut. "I don't know who she is, or how often he sees her, but sometimes I can smell another woman on him."

"Are you sure?" Vicky asked as she tried to look into the woman's eyes. "Maybe he is just picking up perfume from another woman at work."

"Not at the plant," Sandy giggled and shook her head. "None of the men that work there wear anything quite so flowery," she winked at Vicky in an attempt to cover the hurt in her eyes. But Vicky could see through it. She frowned as she patted the woman's hand gently.

"I'm sorry that you're going through this," Vicky murmured.

"Listen to me, blubbering on about myself, and you don't even know me," Sandy shook her head dismissively. "I'm sorry, I guess it's the wine."

"Don't be sorry," Vicky encouraged her as she gave her hand a light squeeze. "Have you thought about confronting him with what you know?"

"For what?" Sandy shrugged. "He'll never admit to it," she pointed out and finished off the last of her wine. "I'm his bread and butter, and I'm sure he's cautious enough never to lose that," she smiled briefly as she glanced at Vicky. "Ah well, I'm sure there are worse things in life. Thank you for listening," she added as she stood up from the table.

"Let me walk you to your room," Vicky suggested as she stood up as well.

"Oh no, please, I'm fine," Sandy laughed a little. "I don't need an escort, but here," she handed Vicky the glass and nodded her head. "Would you mind having the rest of that bottle sent up to me?"

"Not at all," Vicky replied and smiled as she held the door to the lobby open for Sandy to walk through. Vicky walked back towards the kitchen to ask for the bottle of wine to be sent up with the Holsteads' meal. She found Henry adding the final touches to the main dish.

"Henry, can you make sure that the rest of that bottle of chardonnay goes with the Holsteads' lunch?" Vicky asked as she stepped up beside him.

"Sure," Henry nodded with a slight frown.

"Is something wrong?" Vicky asked as Henry was not his usual boisterous self.

"Not really, it's just Peter can be very forgetful sometimes, it gets a little frustrating," he admitted. "I'm sure he'll start paying closer attention soon. I'll make sure the Holsteads get their wine," he added and flashed a smile in Vicky's direction.

"Thanks, Henry," Vicky smiled, but she left the kitchen feeling a little uneasy. She wasn't sure what to think of Peter, but something simply didn't feel right and if Henry was having his doubts, too, then there might be a real issue.

Vicky headed back outside to tidy up the pool area and make sure it was ready for the rest of the day. Once all of the chairs were in place she decided to spend a little time on the porch to clear her mind. It had been invaded by fabric swatches and place settings. As she walked around to the front of the inn she glanced over the grounds. Everything seemed to be as it should be, aside from the fact that the shed door was slightly open. Sometimes it stuck. She walked over to it and gave it a hard shove. When she heard it click shut she knew it was actually closed. Satisfied, she walked the rest of the way to the front porch.

The sun was shining up ahead. It was surprisingly peaceful for this time of day, with little to interrupt the solace of the gardens she walked through, except for the chirping of birds and the trickling sound of the various fountains that were scattered throughout the gardens. Vicky stepped up onto the porch from the side of the inn and walked towards the swing that hung a few feet from the large bay window that let ample sunlight into the main lobby of the inn. She settled into it and closed her eyes.

Vicky drew a deep breath of the slightly moist air which was laced with the scent of the lush foliage that surrounded the inn. Just as she exhaled her cell phone chirped, announcing that she had a text message. She checked the message to find that it was Mitchell checking in with her. She texted back about the spat she had just witnessed, and that she was looking forward to spending some time with him any time he had the chance. The text that he replied with surprised her. It simply said, 'How about right now?'. She glanced up to find a patrol car rolling into the driveway of the inn. She stood up from the swing and smiled as Mitchell stepped out of the car. He was in full uniform. She hadn't seen him in uniform in some time since he had been promoted to detective.

"What's all this about?" she asked as he climbed the steps and wrapped his arms around her. "Not that I'm complaining," she added with a sultry wink as she made a show of looking him over from head to toe.

"I'm complaining," he gritted his teeth, but couldn't hide a smile in reaction to the way she looked at him. "This is Sheriff McDonald's way of teaching me that he's in charge," he shook his head slowly back and forth. "That man really has something against me. The extra shifts I'm covering are patrol shifts. There are plenty of officers to cover them, but he decided I needed to spend a little time in uniform."

"Wow, he's something," Vicky muttered and bit back the colorful language she would prefer to use. She knew that Mitchell was very respectful of his boss, even if they often didn't see eye to eye.

"Honestly, it's not too bad," Mitchell replied as they walked back over to the swing. He sat down beside her and draped his arm around her shoulders. Vicky immediately felt warmed and relaxed by his presence. Mitchell had that effect on her. No matter what was going on in her life, his presence was simply soothing and seemed to put things into perspective for her.

"How can you say that?" Vicky asked as she leaned her head against the curve of his shoulder and looked up into his eyes. "You've worked so hard to earn your new title."

"I have," he agreed as he entangled his hand with hers. "But I don't lose it just because I'm in uniform, and it is a good reminder of what the patrol officers go through. Besides," he grinned as he leaned in closer to her, "it makes it easier for me to keep an eye on Ida."

"Good point," Vicky laughed, her eyes dancing as she did. "I don't know where she comes up with these ideas."

"Me, neither," Mitchell chuckled and shook his head. "But I've heard from some of the other officers that they've spotted her tearing up and down the back roads. So, I'm going to keep a close watch on her."

"Oh, Aunt Ida," Vicky sighed and melted into Mitchell's arms. She felt so comfortable, even though she knew at any moment his radio might buzz to life and he would have to rush off. But she treasured the moment they were sharing in the middle of such a peaceful, early afternoon.

"Vicky? Vicky where are you?" Sarah shouted from inside the inn. The sound of the fear in her sister's voice was enough to instantly propel Vicky up off the swing. She rushed towards the front door. Mitchell was right on her heels as she stepped into the lobby. She was nearly barreled over by her sister who was running for the elevator while shouting the address of the inn into her cell phone.

"Sarah, what's going on?" Vicky asked with wide, fearful eyes. She could tell from the panic in her sister's expression that whatever it was, wasn't good.

"It's Sandy Holstead, she's had an allergic reaction," Sarah gasped out as the elevator doors slid closed.

"Here, we'll take the stairs," Mitchell said without hesitation. They bounded up the stairs that led to the second floor and arrived in the hallway just as Sarah was stepping into the Holsteads' room. She was crouched down beside Sandy when Mitchell and Vicky walked in. Gerald was on his knees with tears trailing down his cheeks.

"Sandy, Sandy, wake up darling," he was moaning as he clutched at her hand with a trembling grasp.

"Where's her EpiPen?" Sarah barked as Mitchell dropped down beside Sandy to check her vital signs and attempt to clear her airway.

"It's here," Gerald mumbled through his tears as he held out the EpiPen.

Mitchell met Vicky's eyes over Sandy's body and shook his head slowly, she was already gone.

"Why didn't you use it?" Sarah asked Gerald sharply. It was rare for Vicky to hear her sister speak in such a harsh tone, but she was feeling the same quick anger rise within her.

"I tried to," he cringed as his hand trembled. "It's, it's," he nearly choked on his words. "It's empty. There was nothing I could do!"

"Empty?" Mitchell demanded suspiciously. "How could it be empty?"

"She must have used it and forgotten to replace it," Gerald sniffled as he wiped at his eyes. "We were in such a rush this morning, she must have just forgotten."

The ambulance had arrived and the EMTs along with two police officers pushed their way into the room.

"Hey, Mitchell, what do we have here?" one of the younger officers asked as he looked over Sandy's body.

"Allergic reaction from what we can tell," Mitchell replied as he stood up and walked over to stand beside Vicky. "Looks like an unfortunate accident."

"Looks like it," Vicky muttered to herself, but her eyes were narrowed. Sarah was doing her best to console Gerald as the EMTs made a futile attempt to revive the woman sprawled out on the floor.

"It must have been something she ate," Gerald said quietly as he stared at the meals that were spread out on the small dining table in the room.

His words drew both Sarah's and Vicky's attention first to each other and then to the plates on the table. Vicky's heartbeat began to quicken.

"But that's impossible we made sure nothing with peanuts..." Vicky began to say, stumbling over her words as she spoke them.

"Not now, Vicky," Sarah said sternly as she wrapped an arm around Gerald's shoulders. Vicky nodded that she understood. This was a time of grief for Gerald, not a time to openly discuss why or how the tragedy had happened. Vicky was still a little in shock as Mitchell led her out of the room.

"What a terrible thing," he said quietly as he hugged her in the hallway. He paused and looked into her eyes. "How are you holding up?"

"This is terrible," Vicky agreed. "But something just doesn't seem right to me." She had never known anyone who was severely allergic to something not to make sure they had an EpiPen ready to go when they needed it. How could Sandy have been so careless as not to make sure she had one with her during a weekend trip?

"Vicky, sometimes an accident is just an accident no matter how tragic it is," Mitchell reminded her calmly. "This will all get sorted out," he assured her.

Vicky nodded and she kept her suspicions quiet as she knew that there was a lot to unravel. After Sarah settled Gerald, she stepped out into the hallway as well.

"We need to have a meeting as soon as possible," Sarah said in a whisper to Vicky and glanced warily at Mitchell. "Alone," she added.

Vicky was surprised at Sarah's tone, and the worry in her sister's eyes.

"I have to go anyway," Mitchell said with a frown. "Sheriff McDonald is going to want to know as much as possible about this," he kissed Vicky lightly on the cheek. "Let me know if either of you need anything," he added as he looked from Vicky to Sarah and back to Vicky again. "You know that I'm here to help."

Despite the fact that Sarah and Mitchell knew each other fairly well, Vicky felt the tension rise between them. It was an emotional situation, Vicky knew, but it bothered her a little that Sarah seemed to be concerned about Mitchell's presence.

"I know," Vicky replied, but she was getting more worried by the moment, especially because of how apprehensive Sarah looked. As Mitchell walked off down the hallway, Vicky turned to Sarah.

"Are you okay?" she asked her with a deep frown.

"I'm not sure," Sarah replied, her voice wavering as she spoke. "This is a very serious problem, Vicky. You need to be careful how much you say to Mitchell," she added.

"Sarah, I trust Mitchell," Vicky said sternly.

"This isn't about trust, Vicky," Sarah explained as patiently as she could. "This is about protecting the inn and ourselves from what is about to turn into a circus."

Slowly it began to dawn on Vicky that Sarah was expecting the inn to take full responsibility for Sandy's death. Vicky hadn't fully considered that.

"Oh, Sarah," Vicky sighed as she ran her fingertips across her forehead and tried to settle the quick anxiety that rushed through her.

"I want you to call Aunt Ida and get her here for a meeting. I want all of us to be on the same page," Sarah said firmly. Though there was panic in her voice, she seemed determined to handle the situation before it got any worse.

"I'll have her meet us in my apartment," Vicky suggested.

"Perfect," Sarah nodded and lowered her voice. "A terrible tragedy has happened here, Vicky, but the circumstances of Mrs. Holstead's death are going to put the inn and everyone who works in it under deep scrutiny."

"I understand," Vicky nodded as her stomach twisted. She felt terrible about Sandy being dead, but it felt even worse to see fear in her older sister's eyes.

Chapter Three

The inn was buzzing with movement as the officers came in, followed by the medical examiner. There wasn't much that Sarah could do to prevent the other guests who were staying at the inn from seeing the commotion that was occurring. She remained at the front desk to answer any questions and explain the situation as well as offering to make arrangements for guests to stay elsewhere if they felt uncomfortable. Vicky called her aunt repeatedly. She was sure that her aunt wasn't answering because she couldn't hear the phone over the roar of the engine of her motorcycle. Vicky was getting more frustrated with every moment that passed as she knew that it was important to Sarah that Aunt Ida be there.

She paced around her small living room as she waited for Aunt Ida to arrive.

"Did you get hold of her?" Sarah asked when she stepped into the apartment a few minutes later.

"I've left a few messages," Vicky replied helplessly. "She must be on her motorcycle."

Sarah rolled her eyes at that. Ida was known for her antics, but buying a motorcycle was taking it further than either Sarah or Vicky had expected.

Sarah perched on the edge of the couch and pretended to be calm. Vicky frowned as she could tell her sister was very out of sorts, no matter how well she was covering it up.

"Sarah, we'll figure this out," she said gently. Before Sarah could answer, they heard the door knob wiggling back and forth. When Ida opened the door to Vicky's apartment she did so with a flourish. She whisked off her leather jacket as she stalked inside revealing a neon-green, tube-top shirt underneath. Sarah didn't even flinch, which led Vicky to believe that she was in a severe state of shock. Vicky couldn't help but admire her aunt's abs of steel with some jealousy.

"Oh, you two look absolutely horrid," Aunt Ida said with a frown as she tossed her jacket onto the back of the couch and dropped down onto the couch beside Sarah. "What are you both so worried about?" she demanded as she looked from one tense expression to the other. "Is this all about my motorcycle?"

"No," Vicky exhaled as she shook her head. "It's not about the motorcycle."

"We have a real problem on our hands, Aunt Ida," Sarah said darkly as she scooted closer to her aunt on the couch and looked up at Vicky. "Sandy Holstead is dead, and it appears to be from an allergic reaction. If there really were peanuts in Sandy's food after she informed us of her allergy then the inn could be held responsible for her death."

"You think that people that rich will sue us?" Aunt Ida asked with surprise and a cluck of her tongue. "Don't they have enough already?"

"It isn't just about money, Aunt Ida," Sarah pointed out with a shake of her head. "It's about recklessness and the fact that a person lost their life because of something someone at this inn did."

"But you don't really believe that do you, Sarah?" Vicky asked as she looked into her sister's eyes.

"I don't know what to think," Sarah admitted with a shake of her head. "We're looking at a situation where it's quite obvious that Sandy ingested peanuts, and the food she consumed was food that had been prepared in our kitchen."

"But you know that Henry never would have allowed peanuts or any products that contain peanuts to go anywhere near her food," Vicky insisted anxiously. She began to pace again in an attempt to keep herself calm. She didn't want to see Henry lose his job over something that she was certain was not his fault. Sarah sighed heavily, her eyes were closed tightly and her lips stretched thin. Vicky could tell from the redness of her cheeks that she was feeling very stressed.

"All I know for sure is that Sandy Holstead is dead, and we're going to have to figure out what happened," Sarah said with a grim frown. "If we're going to save the inn, and save Henry from a possible criminal or civil law suit, then we have to find another explanation for how this happened."

"I still don't understand how she could have forgotten that her EpiPen was used already," Vicky pointed out grimly. "If I was deathly allergic to something, I wouldn't ever forget something like that."

"It is strange," Sarah agreed and then sighed. "But she was on vacation, maybe it somehow slipped her mind. Whatever the reason it did, it doesn't change the fact that something in the food triggered the allergy in the first place," she pointed out.

"Is it possible that it had nothing to do with the food?" Vicky suggested hopefully.

"What do you mean?" Sarah asked curiously.

"Well, maybe she ingested the peanuts in some other way. She had just eaten, but that doesn't mean the peanuts were in her food, does it?" she asked. "Maybe she ingested it in some other way, or maybe her reaction was due to something else entirely."

"Well, the lab will examine the contents of her stomach, as well as the food she was eating, but I guess our first step should be checking the kitchen," Sarah suggested. Her eyes grew a little lighter at the notion that there could be some other explanation for Sandy's death. "But who knows what we will find," Sarah added. "To be honest, if it is our fault, we should take responsibility."

"Nonsense, Sarah, I really doubt that anyone at the inn did this," Vicky said sternly. "I'll check the kitchen," she offered as she saw the stress mounting in her sister's expression again. "You try and get a little rest before the next round of questions, okay?"

"Okay," Sarah sighed with relief. Sarah could handle running the entire inn mostly on her own but facing an investigation into an accidental death was very different from what she was used to.

"I'll come with you," Aunt Ida suggested, it was clear from the gleam in her eyes that the mystery had piqued her interest.

"Fine," Sarah agreed warily. "But Aunt Ida, none of your antics, this is a very delicate matter. Both of you need to be very careful what you say and who you talk to," Sarah warned them before she stretched out on the couch.

"I'll come back to check on you," Vicky promised after draping a throw blanket over her sister.

***

When they stepped out of Vicky's apartment Aunt Ida grabbed Vicky by the arm and looked into her eyes. "Be honest with me here, kiddo, do you think this was a mistake?"

"Not on our part," Vicky shook her head slowly. "You know how careful Sarah is about things. She pays attention to every tiny detail. Henry is very conscientious as well, he would never have let peanuts enter their food."

As they walked towards the kitchen, Aunt Ida spoke to Vicky in a low, soft voice.

"I think you're right about the EpiPen," she said as they nodded to a few guests who were in the lobby while they walked through it. "It doesn't make sense that she wouldn't take the precaution to make sure that she was protected, especially when she was visiting a new place, with no way of knowing how cooperative the staff would be," Ida's words became more rapid as she continued. "She knew how risky it was."

"That's true," Vicky nodded as they turned down the hall that led to the kitchen. "The way she and her husband were fighting, I wouldn't be surprised if he was involved in this. Sandy confided in me that she suspected he was having an affair, of course," Vicky hesitated and frowned. "She'd also had quite a bit of wine at the time. Maybe she was too drunk to realize she hadn't replaced the EpiPen."

"Maybe," Ida replied but still didn't seem convinced. Vicky paused outside the door of the kitchen. She could see Henry hunched over the center island in the middle of the kitchen. His shoulders were trembling, and though his back was to her, Vicky could tell that he was holding a bottle in his hand.

"Poor Henry," she said quietly as she observed the man. Her heart sank as she realized that he was the one who was going to bear the brunt of the accusations. He was so very careful about every meal he created, she knew he would hold himself responsible for Sandy's death. Vicky cleared her throat to announce her presence, and Henry straightened up.

"Henry, we're here to check the kitchen," Vicky said as she stepped into the kitchen with

Ida right behind her. "We just want to make sure that there were no peanuts or peanut products left in here, even though I know you cleaned it all out this morning."

"Don't bother," Henry said huskily as he continued to stand with his back to them.

"What do you mean?" Vicky asked as she moved closer to him and saw that it wasn't just his shoulders that were shaking, it was his entire body.

"I mean, I already know how the peanuts got into Mrs. Holstead's food," he whispered, his voice barely audible despite the fact that Vicky was standing right behind him.

"Henry, what are you saying?" Ida asked as she made sure the door was closed and then stepped up beside him as well.

"It said sunflower oil," he gasped out as he reluctantly turned to face them. He had tears streaming down his cheeks as he looked from Ida to Vicky. "See?" he held up the bottle he was clutching so tightly in his right hand that his knuckles were white. It was a tan, decorative bottle for storing oil. A neatly printed label declared that the bottle contained sunflower oil. Henry labeled everything in his kitchen to ensure that anything he created had the right ingredients.

"And?" Vicky whispered almost afraid to ask as her eyes widened. "It wasn't sunflower oil?"

"No," he exhaled as fresh tears poured down his cheeks. "No, it wasn't sunflower oil," he opened the cap of the bottle and the distinct scent of peanut oil wafted up under their noses.

"Oh no," Vicky winced and took a step back as she placed her finger under her nose. It wasn't the smell she found offensive, but the consequences of the peanut oil being stored in the wrong bottle that disturbed her.

"Didn't you smell it?" Ida demanded with frustration as she glowered at Henry. "Anyone can smell that and know that it's not sunflower oil!"

"I did!" he insisted, fresh tears forming and his grief causing his voice to crack. "In fact just to be extra cautious I emptied out all of the sunflower oil that was in here, I cleaned the bottle, and refilled it with sunflower oil myself!" he shook his head as he stared at the offending bottle with a mixture of shock and hatred. "I know I did."

"So, you're saying someone else must have put the peanut oil in the bottle after you cleaned and refilled it?" Vicky asked as she studied the bottle intently. There was no sign that it had been tampered with, but it wasn't a sealed bottle and the cap just screwed off so there was no way to tell what had happened to it.

"Someone must have," Henry insisted as he handed the bottle to Vicky so she could have a closer look. "I know for a fact there was no peanut oil in there, not even when I added the oil to the food. In fact there wasn't a trace of peanut oil in this kitchen. Someone had to bring it in from outside the kitchen. But that's just crazy, isn't it?" he shook his head as if he was doubting himself.

Vicky was certain as she rolled the bottle between her fingers that Henry was telling the truth, but Ida didn't look as convinced.

"Or maybe you just made a mistake," Ida pointed out and shook her head. "And now you've covering it up because you know the inn and you will be held responsible."

"Aunt Ida!" Vicky frowned as she shot a glare in her direction. "Henry wouldn't do that!"

"Maybe not," Ida said with a sigh. "But that is what the police are going to say when they find peanut oil in Sandy's food."

"If that were the case why would I admit to it now?" he snapped in return. "Why would I suddenly say there was peanut oil in the wrong bottle? I would never lie about something like that!"

"Calm down, Henry," Vicky cringed as she glanced towards the entrance of the kitchen and then back to him. "Just keep this quiet for now," she slid the bottle of oil into her pocket.

"Vicky, what are you doing?" Aunt Ida hissed as she stared at her niece. "You can't conceal evidence! If anyone finds out, you could face jail time!"

"It isn't real evidence," Vicky argued in return, though she was careful to keep her voice low. "It's evidence that was planted, to make it look as if this death was accidental. But Sandy's death was no accident," she said grimly as she looked from Henry to Ida. "Sandy Holstead was murdered. I'm not going to let Henry be accused of something he didn't do, and I'm not going to let the inn take the fall because someone decided it was the perfect place to commit a murder. It may seem like the wrong thing to do, Aunt Ida, but it's the only thing I can think of right now. Until we get to the bottom of this, all three of us have to be clear on one thing," she looked from one face to the other. "This bottle never existed, understand?"

Henry swallowed thickly, he still had tears in his eyes, but he nodded. Aunt Ida sighed heavily, she wrung her hands together and shook her head with frustration.

"Yes, Vicky," she finally agreed.

"I need to speak with Henry," a voice said from right behind Vicky. Vicky spun on her heel to find a tall man in an expensive, black business suit staring hard at her. For just a moment Vicky was startled by his hawk-like gaze and his fierce stance. He was a slender man, to the point of being called skinny, but his presence was very large and full of arrogance. When Vicky found her voice again Ida had stepped closer to her.

"May I ask who you are?" Vicky inquired in a polite tone.

"My name is Barry Baker. I am a lawyer, and I represent the Lambard family," he said as he studied Vicky. "I don't need to know who you are, I already do. You and your sister own this inn. Now, if you don't mind, I need to speak with Henry alone."

"I'm sorry, I'm not sure that would be best..." Vicky began to say.

"I'm sorry, I didn't mean to give you the impression that you had a choice," Barry responded and narrowed his eyes. Ida moved closer to him, her gaze locking with his.

"Listen Barry, we're all trying to understand what happened here. Perhaps I can interest you in a glass of ice water?" she offered, and batted her eyelids flirtatiously. Barry seemed to be distracted by Ida's behavior, and the corners of his lips even turned upward slightly. Vicky was shocked at how quickly they had arranged for a lawyer to come.

"Water would be nice," he agreed with a slight nod. As Aunt Ida sashayed across the kitchen to retrieve the water, Barry turned back to Vicky. "Please excuse us," he said sternly.

"I'm not going anywhere," Vicky retorted growing more annoyed by the moment.

"It's okay, Vicky," Ida insisted as she brought Barry his ice water. "I'll keep this strapping, young man company while he talks to Henry," she purred as she drifted her fingertips along the back of Barry's hand. "You don't mind, do you, Mr. Baker?" she asked and offered a seductive gaze.

"Well, I suppose it couldn't do any harm," he chuckled and watched Ida as he took a sip of his ice water. Vicky knew that Ida would keep a close eye on the situation, and she needed to warn Sarah about the lawyer's presence. She looked up at Henry who was starting to pull himself together. She met his eyes as she spoke to Barry.

"I think you'll find no matter what questions you ask, the inn is not responsible for Mrs. Holstead's death. In fact, your time might be better spent finding out who exactly her husband was having an affair with," she suggested and then shifted her gaze slowly to Barry.

"Ha," Barry smirked as he glanced over at Vicky. "If I spent my time tracking down mistresses I'd never have time for anything else. I'm not interested in affairs. Mrs. Holstead died of an allergic reaction, one she no doubt informed your staff about. Now, I want to know how this happened. Her family is expecting an answer, and I certainly will give them one," he furrowed a heavy brow as he met Vicky's eyes directly. "Now, if I have to ask you again to excuse us, then I will have to launch an even more thorough investigation into whether you were trying to withhold evidence of negligence. Perhaps we should get local law enforcement involved?" he suggested.

Vicky swallowed thickly. She could feel the bottle of oil pressing against the inside of her pocket. She knew that if Barry, or even worse, Mitchell discovered that she was hiding it, she would be in serious legal trouble.

"Yes, sir, please excuse me," she said quietly and stepped out of the kitchen. She hurried down the hall to her apartment and opened it to find Sarah just about to open the door from the other side. "Sarah, the Lambard family lawyer is here," she gasped out in one breath.

"I know," Sarah frowned. "Michelle is working the front desk, she texted me to let me know that he'd arrived. I need to get to him fast..."

"Sarah, wait," Vicky grabbed her by the elbow and steered her back into her apartment. "You need to listen to me. He's questioning Henry right now."

"That's okay," Sarah shrugged and tried not to panic. "I know Henry wasn't involved in this so..."

"Sarah," Vicky growled and pulled the bottle of oil out of her pocket. "I know he wasn't either, but someone is trying to make it look like he was. Whoever put the peanut oil in this bottle, was not just trying to kill Sandy, but also trying to frame Henry for the crime."

"Oh no," Sarah gasped when she caught the scent of the peanut oil. "This is terrible! Do you think Henry is going to tell the lawyer that he made a mistake?"

"Henry is very honest," Vicky said and bit into her bottom lip. She wasn't sure what Henry would do, especially in his emotional state. "What we need is a good distraction, we need to get Henry away from Barry Baker, and everyone out of the kitchen."

"The fire alarm," Sarah suggested, her eyes widening. "We can set off the fire alarm, then maybe we can get them out of the kitchen."

"No, it needs to be more than that," Vicky said as she tried to come up with something that would absolutely drive everyone out of the kitchen.

"The sprinkler system," she announced suddenly. "Barry was wearing an expensive suit, if the sprinklers go off he's going to run out of that kitchen."

"But the sprinklers only go off if there's smoke," Sarah pointed out with a shake of her head. "We can't just turn them on."

"Don't worry about it, Sarah. You go to the front desk, I'll take care of the sprinklers, understand?" she met her sister's eyes.

"Vicky, please be careful. Whatever you do, get that bottle out of your pocket and put it in a safe place!" she hissed. "If you get caught with it…"

"Sarah, everything is going to be fine," Vicky declared impatiently. But as her sister brushed past her and Vicky rummaged through her kitchen drawer for a lighter, she had no idea if everything was really going to be fine.

Chapter Four

Vicky knew that she needed to get back inside the kitchen. Unfortunately, when she peeked into the kitchen she saw that Aunt Ida, Barry, and Henry were all standing around the island in the center of the room. There was no way to get inside without them noticing. If she slipped inside and then the sprinklers went off Barry would be very suspicious. She decided that the only way she was going to get inside was through a window.

Vicky stepped out through one of the side doors towards the gardens and walked around to the staff quarters. The staff quarters were directly across from the kitchen, with a walkway and large, grassy space between them. There was only one window on the wall of the kitchen facing the staff quarters that was large enough for her to fit through. It was a window into the pantry. Vicky tried to jump up high enough to grab it but it was a high window. Instead, she had to drag one of the rubber trash cans around from behind the kitchen and place it beneath the kitchen window. She tested its strength with one foot. It was tough rubber, but it was still rubber. She balanced herself by leaning her hand on the brick surface of the outside wall as she climbed up onto the trash can.

The center of the lid of the trash can began to give way, making her feel as if she was going to fall through it. She gripped the ledge tightly, worried that she might fall and cause a commotion. Just as the trash can was about to give way completely, Vicky managed to get the window open. She tossed one leg over the windowsill and then climbed the rest of the way in. When she got both legs on the other side of the windowsill she encountered a new problem. The floor of the pantry was a long way down. Luckily, there was a small ladder that was used to reach the items on the highest shelves of the pantry. She managed to hook her foot through one of the rungs and guide it closer to her. Once it was stable against the wall she climbed the rest of the way through the window. She could hear the voices in the kitchen, and though they were muffled she could tell that Henry's voice was full of defeat. It seemed as if he was preparing to make a confession.

There was nothing Vicky could do but hope that her paper and lighter would be enough to convince the sprinklers there was a large fire. She stood on the ladder in the pantry, nearly tumbling off it every time she tried to ignite the lighter. In the kitchen she could hear the voices of Barry and Henry growing a little louder.

"Do you often use peanuts in the food?" Barry asked.

"Of course I do," he replied with a heavy sigh. "It's a common ingredient in its different forms in many of the meals that I prepare."

"And were you informed of Sandy Holstead's allergy to peanuts?" he asked. From the next equally deep sigh that Henry produced, Vicky knew that he had already surrendered himself to the idea that it was his fault.

"Yes, I was," he replied reluctantly.

"So, you're the one who prepares all the food?" Barry asked.

"I am," Henry replied morosely. "With some assistance from my sous chef."

"And where is he?" Barry pressed, his tone becoming more insistent.

"I- I," Henry stammered for a moment. "I honestly don't know," he finally said. "But he wasn't involved in this. I was the one who made the food."

Vicky winced as she knew that if Henry continued to give Barry evidence against him there was going to be a real problem clearing his name. She flicked the lighter three times in a row and finally got a flame. She touched the flame to the edge of the piece of paper and then held the paper up towards the sprinkler head. What she didn't expect was how fast the paper began to burn. She cringed as the heat quickly approached her fingertips. She swayed on the ladder as the top half of the paper became hot ash that fell against the skin on the back of her hand. Just when the flame was about to touch her fingertips the sprinkler finally came to life and began spraying the paper, and of course, Vicky. All of the sprinklers in the kitchen began spraying. The system was designed to work so that the sprinklers in the kitchen were the only ones to go off, but the fire alarm was triggered throughout the inn. As Vicky had hoped, Barry began to complain about his suit.

"Ugh, what's this?" he demanded. "My suit. We have to get out of here!"

"Don't worry, Barry, come this way," Ida suggested and pulled him out through the back door of the kitchen. Henry took his opportunity to escape the questioning and went out through the interior entrance of the kitchen into the hallway. Vicky waited until she was sure that Barry, Ida, and Henry were out of the kitchen, then she made her way down the slippery rungs of the ladder. She nearly lost her footing on the last rung, but managed to keep her balance long enough to fall backwards on a large sack of flour. The sack was open and some of the white powder plumed upwards, coating Vicky's damp shirt and pants. She hurried out of the pantry and out into the hallway outside the kitchen. Henry was nowhere in sight, but Sarah was quickly approaching down the hallway.

"Vicky, are you okay?" she asked quickly.

"I am," Vicky whispered back. "Just make sure that Barry talks to you before he talks to Henry again, okay?"

"Okay," Sarah nodded and hurried back to the front desk. Vicky wanted to find Henry and tell him to remain quiet, but first she needed to change out of her damp, flour-covered clothes. The only problem was in order to get to her apartment she had to walk through the lobby, or risk going outside and around the pool, where Barry might see her. She opted for the outside option so that she wouldn't track flour through the lobby. As soon as she stepped outside she regretted it. Ida and Barry were standing in the garden where there was plenty of afternoon sun to dry off his clothing.

Vicky tried to duck back inside, but Barry was a keen observer and he heard the door open before she could close it again.

"Vicky?" he called out as he saw her soaked clothing. "You weren't in the kitchen," he pointed out suspiciously and began walking towards her. "Did you have something to do with all of this?"

"What?" Vicky shot back with frustration. "Of course not. I went to the kitchen to check on the three of you, but you were already gone."

"What is this you're covered in?" Barry asked as he touched her shoulder and stared down at his fingertip covered in white powder.

"Oh, Vicky, did you slip?" Ida asked quickly when she saw Vicky's blank look. "Are you hurt?"

"I slipped," Vicky nodded with a smile of relief. "But I'm okay. I landed on the bag of flour, luckily," she added.

"How very lucky," Barry replied through gritted teeth. Vicky could tell that he wasn't buying any of it. But there was no way he could prove what she had done, especially since the entire kitchen had been thoroughly washed by the sprinklers. Unfortunately, that also meant that any clues Vicky might have been able to find about who really killed Sandy Holstead were washed away as well.

"Where is your sister?" Barry asked as he settled his gaze on her.

"She's at the front desk," Vicky replied with a mild shrug. "I'm sure she's waiting to talk with you."

"I'm sure you've already told her I'm here," Barry replied with a grim smile. Vicky allowed Barry to get a few steps ahead of her. Then she decided to follow after him. She wanted to see how Sarah reacted to his presence. Vicky followed close behind Barry but did her best to keep her footsteps muffled. She heard him as he walked up to the front desk.

"Hello, I need to speak with Sarah," he said calmly as he stood in front of the desk.

"I'm Sarah," she replied and Vicky could hear the smile in her voice.

"Is there somewhere we could speak in private?" he suggested after introducing himself.

"Sure," Sarah agreed. Vicky knew she would lead Barry into her office which was just behind the front desk. As much as she wanted to hear what Barry asked, she knew that Sarah could handle the questions. She also wanted to change, but she didn't want to miss the opportunity to get to Sandy's room. This was her best chance to get up to Sandy's room and have another look around before Barry began his investigation. The police still considered Sandy's death to be accidental, now that Vicky was certain it had been intentional, she was hoping there would be some clues in her room.

When Vicky reached the Holsteads' room she found it in disarray. It looked as if someone had tossed every piece of clothing from their suitcases around the room. The bedding was stripped and tossed on the floor. She wondered if she was too late and if Barry had already been inside. As she picked through the clothing in an attempt to find some clues, she found a fork on the floor. It was a fork from the kitchen. Vicky used one of the pillow cases that had been tossed on the floor to pick it up. She looked at it closely. She could see a sheen of oil on it.

Not far from the fork was the bottle of wine that Sandy had asked to be sent up to her. When Vicky picked it up she found something stuck underneath it. It was a receipt stuck to the bottom by the condensation on the bottle. It was a receipt from the local diner. It showed a total of just over ten dollars and it appeared to be for a meal for only one person. Why would there be a receipt from the local diner if on their first meal at the inn they had room service for lunch? She tucked it into her pocket and started to turn around to leave the room, when a shadow fell across the carpet. She looked up slowly to discover Henry standing just outside the door.

"Vicky, I just, I had to see the room…" he said quietly, his words cut off by a strangled gasp.

"Henry," Vicky said his name sharply in an attempt to snap him out of the dazed state he was in. "This was not your fault," she said with determination as she looked into his eyes. "Whoever is responsible for Sandy's death did it intentionally, this was no accident."

"But the bottle…" he began to say.

"Henry, I'm telling you right now, say nothing more until we can figure out exactly what has happened, understand?" she searched his gaze hoping that her words had reached him through the shock that he was obviously experiencing.

"I want nothing more to do with this," he stated flatly and shook his head. "I won't deny my mistake. If I did this, then I should be punished!"

"But you didn't!" Vicky said impatiently as she narrowed her eyes. "You know you didn't, and so do I, Henry, why would you risk your future when you were not involved?"

"No matter what, I must have been the one to put the oil on her food," he said in a whisper with tears in his eyes.

"That's not necessarily the case," Vicky argued the point and steered him away from the Holsteads' room. "I want you to go to your room. Stay in it, don't answer your phone, don't answer your door. Only come out if it's me or Sarah, understand?" she locked eyes with him.

"Yes, I understand," he nodded but his eyes were still clouded with tears. Vicky left the room as quickly as she entered it. She didn't want to be there if Barry Baker decided to look it over. She headed back to her own apartment to change her wet, flour-covered clothes. When she reached the door of her apartment she found a man standing in front of it. He didn't look like an average guest at the inn, he was very tall and very wide. His hair was gray and curly. It hung several inches past his shoulders against a brown leather jacket.

"Can I help you?" Vicky asked hesitantly as she stepped up behind him. The man turned to look at her, and his brown eyes widened when he saw the state of her clothing.

"Wow, looks like you're having a bad day," his voice was raspy and full of humor.

"Not the best, that's for sure," Vicky replied, a little more at ease because of his cheerful attitude.

"I'm looking for Ida," he explained as he shoved his thick hands into the pockets of his jeans. "She said that she lived here but..."

"Why are you looking for her?" Vicky asked suspiciously. With the strange situations her aunt could get herself into she wasn't sure how much she should tell the man.

"Oh, I wanted to invite her to dinner," he explained shyly and Vicky detected a blush in his cheeks. Despite everything unfolding around her,

Vicky found his bashfulness to be endearing, and the fact that he was looking for Aunt Ida did not surprise her in the least.

"Well, she's probably in her room, let me give her a call," Vicky suggested and started to reach for her cell phone until she realized it was in her sopping wet pocket.

"That's all right, I'll call her," he chuckled and shook his head. "I'm Rex by the way, if you see her before I do, just tell her I'll be by her beauty in the parking lot."

"I will," Vicky grinned as she watched him walk away. Of all the men that she had seen Aunt Ida flirt with, he was the first biker. She had to wonder what came first, Rex or the motorcycle.

***

Once Vicky had changed she headed back to the lobby hoping to catch up with Aunt Ida to ask her about Rex. Instead she came across Sarah and Barry standing by the door of the inn talking in tense voices.

"Something happened here," he was saying sharply. "It doesn't matter what you claim, what it comes down to is that there must have been peanuts on Sandy Holstead's food, prepared and served at this inn, after she informed you of her allergy."

"As I said, we took every precaution to prevent any peanuts getting into her food..." Sarah began to argue in return.

"Obviously not," Barry snapped back as Vicky walked over to the two.

"Have you considered the possibility that Gerald was the one to add peanuts to his wife's food?" Vicky asked in an attempt to take the pressure off her sister for a moment. "Just because the peanuts might be found on Mrs. Holstead's food that doesn't mean that it wasn't added after the meals were delivered to the room."

Barry spun around so fast to face Vicky that she gasped in reaction to the movement. "Are you accusing a grieving widower of poisoning his wife?" he demanded and took a step towards Vicky.

"No, of course not," Sarah said quickly and stepped between them. "What Vicky is trying to say is that there are many possibilities. We don't know exactly what happened just yet. A thorough investigation should and will be conducted."

"Yes," Barry replied in a seething tone as he looked at Vicky. "It will."

He pushed past both of them and stepped out the door of the inn.

"Doesn't sound like that went too well," Vicky said grimly as she watched Barry stalk off to his car.

"He certainly is determined," Sarah said with a sigh as she walked around behind the desk.

"Well, I'm not going to leave your side anymore," Vicky said as she shook her head. She would have to postpone her meeting with Melissa, the waitress who was having her bridal shower at the inn on the weekend. "I don't like the way that he was talking to you."

Sarah offered a fond smile but shook her head as she spoke. "Listen Vicky, the best way to keep our reputation intact is to continue to operate as normal. If you don't show up for the meeting with Melissa, then everyone in town will think that we're circling the wagons and trying to avoid taking responsibility for Sandy's death," she pointed out and shuffled the papers on her desk. "Barry Baker means business, and if we're not very careful he's going to make sure this inn is shut down," Sarah warned.

"But how can I plan a bridal shower with all of this happening?" Vicky asked as she leaned against the desk and studied her sister. "Do you really think I can pick out colors and suggest cakes?"

"Of course you can," Sarah said with a smile of confidence. "You can do anything you put your mind to."

"If you think it's what's best," Vicky said quietly as she recalled the receipt she had found on the floor in the Holsteads' room. It was for the diner where Melissa was a waitress. Maybe she could find out some information about who had eaten there.

"I think it's what we need to do for now," Sarah pursed her lips as she looked over the list of new guests that would be arriving the next day. "We need the inn to run as smoothly as possible. If we have any more incidents while Barry is here, we're just going to look more and more incapable of providing a safe environment."

"All right," Vicky reluctantly agreed. She hesitated for a moment before adding in a whisper. "Just to let you know there's a burly biker wandering around here looking for Aunt Ida."

"You're kidding me!" Sarah burst out laughing and covered her mouth quickly. Vicky smiled at the light that filled her sister's eyes. It was good to hear her laugh, even if it did draw a few looks from some of the staff members within earshot.

"He wants to ask her out to dinner," Vicky added with a gleam in her eye. "I think Aunt Ida has him wrapped around her little finger."

"You think?" Sarah laughed quietly. "I'm certain of it!"

Vicky was still smiling as she walked out of the inn to her car.

Chapter Five

The diner was not too far from the inn. It was located along one of the highways that connected Highland with some of the larger nearby cities. Even though it was nothing special, it was a popular place for those who commuted. When Vicky pulled into the parking lot there weren't a lot of other cars. It was a little early for dinner and far too late for lunch. That was why Melissa had chosen that time to meet with Vicky, as she felt it would be slow enough for them to go over some details.

Vicky didn't know Melissa too well other than to say hello if she passed her on the street, but she was impressed by how much she managed to juggle. As she prepared for her wedding to a man who worked as a mechanic in Highland, she also worked long hours and tended to her grandparents. Vicky was happy when Melissa had been the one chosen for the free bridal shower, and the best part was that she and Sarah had decided to take it a step further and offer Melissa the inn as the venue for her wedding. Melissa didn't know that yet, they were going to surprise her at her bridal shower.

As Vicky walked into the diner, she felt a sinking sensation in her stomach. If things continued to go as they were, Melissa might never get that surprise. The thought reminded her of the receipt in her pocket. She pulled it out of her pocket and smoothed it down. Vicky studied the receipt. She looked at the different prices listed on it, and the name that was signed at the bottom of the credit card receipt attached. It had taken some time to figure out who had signed the receipt, because it was wet and the signature consisted of an initial and the name Holstead. But it was fairly clear to Vicky now, that it had been the initial G for Gerald. When she stepped further inside the diner she discovered that Melissa was standing behind the counter pouring some drinks for customers.

"Hi, Melissa," Vicky said as cheerfully as she could. She wanted to keep up appearances as Sarah had requested.

"Oh, hi, Vicky, I wasn't sure if you'd be coming," she said in a rush. "Just give me a moment, okay?"

"Sure, take as long as you need," Vicky assured her and took a seat at the counter. There were ten bar stools lined up at the counter, and on a few of them there were locals perched. Two gave Vicky sidelong looks. Vicky could tell that rumors must have already been flying through town about what had happened at the inn earlier that day. Vicky did her best to ignore the stares, but the more she ignored them, the more obvious they became. Vicky knew that if the inn was held responsible for Sandy's death, they were going to lose a lot of customers, and potentially a lot of friends in town.

"Can I get you something to drink, Vicky?" Melissa asked when she returned to the counter.

"Just a water with lemon would be good," Vicky requested with a smile. As Melissa returned with her water, Vicky leaned in close to her.

"Have you noticed anyone from out of town in the diner lately?" Vicky asked her hesitantly. She didn't want to be completely open about questioning Melissa about Gerald, as she felt it would once more stir up the gossip mill.

"Well, we do get some truckers that pass through," Melissa pointed out and then lowered her voice as she leaned a little closer to Vicky. "Why is there some kind of celebrity lurking around incognito?" she asked with a sparkle in her eyes.

"No, not exactly," Vicky replied with a frown. "Any chance you know who might have been the waitress who served this customer?" Vicky asked as she slid the receipt towards Melissa.

Melissa picked up the receipt and glanced over it swiftly. "Sure, each server has their own code that they enter when they ring a customer up on the register, and that code gets printed on the receipt," Melissa explained and pointed out a two digit code on the bottom of the receipt. "Let me just check that," she walked over to the register and ran her finger down a list of codes that was taped to the front of the register. When she walked back, her eyelids had drooped and she sucked her bottom lip underneath her top row of teeth. She looked fairly concerned as she sat the receipt back down on the counter.

"This is Carolyn's code," she said in a murmur.

"Carolyn?" Vicky repeated as she didn't recognize the name. She knew just about everyone who worked at the diner.

"She's fairly new to town and to the diner," Melissa explained with clear annoyance in her tone. "And honestly I hope she won't last too long. She's obviously never had any serving experience."

"That's got to be tough," Vicky said sympathetically. "Are you training her?"

"I'm trying," Melissa said through gritted teeth. She tilted her head towards a young woman in the corner of the diner. "She spends more time on her cell phone than she does doing anything else."

"Hmm," Vicky nodded as she watched the woman tapping away at the screen of her cell phone. "I can see why you would be frustrated."

"I've tried talking to her, but she's not the friendly type," Melissa shrugged.

"Okay, well, why don't we get started on the plans for your bridal shower?" Vicky suggested with a smile, though she kept an eye on Carolyn. She found it interesting that Carolyn was so new and yet not the least bit interested in making an impression or following the policies of the diner.

"Sure, there's a table over there by the kitchen that will give us some privacy," Melissa said happily. Vicky nodded and picked up her glass of water. She carried it along with her. Once they were seated, Vicky tried to focus on the details of the bridal shower, but she was feeling very uneasy. She knew that Henry was beside himself and was still locked up in his room, but she wondered how long it would be before his guilty conscience got the better of him. If he admitted to having the bottle of oil and someone found it stowed in Vicky's apartment, she would be in a lot of trouble.

"Vicky?" Melissa asked hesitantly. "Are you listening?" she asked.

"I'm sorry," Vicky shook her head to clear her mind. "What were you saying?" she asked.

"I'd like my bridesmaids to be included in some of the activities, if that's okay," Melissa said with a small smile. "We're all so close, and I don't want them to be left out."

"Oh, of course," Vicky nodded and pointed to a list of activities she had made that involved the bride and her bridesmaids. "How do these sound to you?" she asked. As Melissa was looking over the list, Vicky's eyes wandered over the restaurant. It was an average diner with a few historical pictures of Highland hanging on the walls. There wasn't too much that stood out. But Vicky noticed Carolyn standing behind the counter. She was glowering in their direction.

"Is she one of your bridesmaids?" Vicky asked without thinking about it first.

"Who?" Melissa glanced up in the direction that Vicky was looking. "Oh, Carolyn?" she frowned and lowered her voice as she looked back at Vicky. "I asked her to be, you know out of courtesy because I had asked all of the other waitresses, but we're not very close. She threw a fit when I asked her, told me I was being insensitive," she rolled her eyes dismissively. "I like all of these activities," she added as she looked back down at the list.

"Good," Vicky smiled and made a note on her clipboard. As casually as she could she brought up Carolyn again. "What did she mean about you being insensitive?" Vicky asked, still a little unsettled by the heat of the woman's gaze that seemed to be fixated in their direction.

"Oh, she's in this dead end relationship," Melissa confessed in a murmur. "She's dating a married man, and keeps thinking he's going to leave his wife for her. Of course we all know that routine. We've tried to talk to her about it, but if anyone even suggests that maybe the guy isn't as interested as she thinks, she loses it. Personally, I think she's a little off balance. But, since she can't get married, I guess she thinks anyone who can is rubbing it in her face," Melissa sighed and glanced over at Carolyn then looked back at Vicky. "I really wasn't. I was just trying to be nice."

"Of course, you were," Vicky nodded. "Trust me you're better off not having included her. You want to surround yourself with people who have your best interests at heart on your special day."

"I agree with that," Melissa smiled and added in a warmer voice. "I can't thank you enough for doing this, Vicky. All of these fancy things, I never expected any of this."

"Well, you deserve it, Melissa," Vicky said sternly. "So, just enjoy it."

"Thanks, Vicky," she smiled again and then stood up from the table. "The dinner rush is about to start, but if you need me for anything just let me know."

"I will," Vicky promised as she began to gather her things together. Once she was ready to leave she noticed that Carolyn was still staring at her. Vicky felt uncomfortable as she walked out of the diner. As she was walking to her car, Aunt Ida's motorcycle roared up beside her. Vicky paused and smiled with admiration as her aunt easily hopped off the motorcycle and pulled off her helmet.

"Vicky, how is everything going at the inn?" she asked quickly.

"I don't know. I'm about to go find out," Vicky explained. "Did Rex find you?" Vicky asked and wiggled her eyebrows.

"Oh," Ida blushed and Vicky tried not to grin. "Yes, I'm meeting him for dinner," she admitted.

"Good for you," Vicky gave her a gentle hug. "Just be careful, okay?" she met her aunt's eyes.

"Vicky," Aunt Ida planted her hands on her hips and stared directly into her niece's eyes. "I have been taking care of myself for longer than you have been alive. I will be just fine."

"I know, I know," Vicky sighed and shook her head as she swept her gaze over the motorcycle Aunt Ida was standing next to. "But I don't want to see you get hurt."

"The only way I'm going to get hurt is if I don't get something to eat, and fast," Aunt Ida laughed. "I've been running around so much today I forgot to have much of anything to eat."

"Well, you're in the right place then," Vicky assured her, winked, and then climbed into her car. As she drove back towards the inn she couldn't help but think of the romantic dinner her aunt was about to share with Rex and it made her even more irritated at Sheriff McDonald.

Chapter Six

Aunt Ida ordered her favorite chocolate malt and sat back in her favorite booth. She spent a lot of time at the diner as she loved to people watch. But today she was looking forward to her first date with Rex, a biker she had met on the road. He was a bit younger than her, with a full beard and wild brown eyes. She had never dated a biker before, and was looking forward to sharing a nice meal with him. As she waited, the two waitresses behind the counter seemed to be having a bit of an argument.

"All I'm saying is I wouldn't want to have my bridal shower at a place where someone just died," the dark haired waitress was saying. She had an attitude to the way she stood, the way she talked, even the way she tilted her head to the side.

"It's certainly nothing to be worried about," the other waitress, who Ida recognized as

Melissa replied. "It was an allergic reaction, an accident after all."

"A pretty serious one!" the first waitress stated. "I mean, how good can the place really be if the chef fed a guest something that killed her?"

"Cut it out, Carolyn," Melissa warned with annoyance growing in her voice. "Sarah and Vicky have been nothing but nice to me. You're just jealous because you're never going to get to have a bridal shower!"

Carolyn's eyes narrowed and she gripped a fork that was on the counter as if she might use it as a weapon.

"We'll just see about that," Carolyn growled. "It won't be long before you're eating your words, Melissa, while you have your little rinky dink wedding, I'll be marrying in Paris with royalty in attendance. Just wait."

"You really are crazy, aren't you?" Melissa spat back with obvious frustration.

"She's not crazy," a voice said sharply from the entrance of the diner. Ida ducked down when she noticed that it was the new sous chef from the inn. He walked up to Carolyn and paused beside her. "Don't talk to my sister like that," he warned Melissa with roughness in his voice. Ida braced herself, prepared to intervene if she needed to.

"You need to wise up, Peter," Melissa warned him and shook her head. "The only reason she even still has a job here is because the owner is friends with you. You know that," she added with a growl.

"Keep your nose out of things that don't have anything to do with you, Melissa," Peter snapped back and Ida abruptly decided that she didn't like this man at all. She made a note to speak to Sarah about him when she returned to the inn. As she continued to listen in, she heard him speak in a quieter tone to his sister.

"Carolyn," he murmured as he pulled her aside.

"How did it go?" Carolyn asked eagerly. "Did you do everything as I asked?"

"Shh," Peter hissed and tugged Carolyn further away from the others in the diner.

They ended up standing right on the other side of Ida's booth which looked empty while she was ducked down.

"It's done," he said in a whisper to Carolyn as she stood close to him.

"Yes!" Carolyn said gleefully. "I'm so excited," Carolyn squealed and clapped her hands. "It's only a matter of time now. I can't wait to see him! Did you see him?" she asked, her voice shrill as she spoke.

"I didn't, but there's a bit of a problem," Peter said in an even lower voice. "There's going to be an investigation."

"Of course there will be," Carolyn cleared her throat. "That snooty woman will be a thorn in my side, even after she's dead!"

"Just be careful, Carolyn," Peter warned sharply. "I put a lot on the line to make this happen for you."

"I will be," Carolyn replied happily. "Don't worry so much, once everything settles we'll never see this town again." As she and Peter walked away their voices faded.

***

Ida could barely believe what she had just heard. Unfortunately, she was sure that the police wouldn't believe it either. She needed to get proof that Peter and Carolyn had been involved in Sandy's death. She left money on her table for her malt and then rushed out of the diner. She quickly called Rex on the way to the parking lot and left a message to meet her at the inn instead of the diner.

Once in the parking lot Aunt Ida hopped onto her motorcycle. As she was speeding down the road towards the inn, her mind was going a million miles a minute. It made sense that Peter would have been able to add the peanut oil to the food. But even knowing this, she couldn't think of a way to pin it directly on him. As her mind spun through different ideas, her motorcycle was trying to keep up. She didn't realize how fast she was going, nor was she paying very close attention to the road. She didn't see the turtle making its slow pilgrimage across the road until she was nearly on top of it. She swerved hard to avoid striking it, and swayed on the motorcycle for a moment before regaining control of it.

What Aunt Ida also didn't see was Mitchell's patrol car nestled in some trees on the side of the road. Mitchell turned on his sirens and lights as Ida buzzed right by him on her motorcycle. She looked in the rear view mirror and groaned as she saw him speeding up to follow after her. At first Ida considered just going faster, but she knew that would not end well. When Mitchell flashed his headlights at her she finally pulled over to the side of the road. She watched through the mirror as Mitchell stepped out of the car and adjusted the hat on top of his head. He walked deliberately towards her.

"Do you know how fast you were going, Ida?" he asked as he tipped his hat back to meet her eyes. It was hard to do because Ida had dark sunglasses that were blocking her eyes. She regarded him with tightened lips and an air of annoyance.

"It's important, Mitchell, I need to get back to the inn as fast as possible," she began to say more, then she remembered Sarah's warning to be careful what she said. She couldn't risk putting the inn in a position where it might be held responsible for Sandy's death. If Mitchell knew anything about the crime he would have to tell his boss all about it.

"Nothing is as important as your life, Ida," he said firmly as he pulled out his ticket book.

"Aw, that's so sweet," Ida replied and pulled off her sunglasses so she could bat her long, dark lashes at him. "I've learned my lesson, Mitchell, really."

"No, I don't think you have," he said sternly as he ignored her flirting. He knew Ida well enough to recognize her antics. "If anything ever happened to you it would devastate your nieces, and I can't stand by and watch you take so many chances by speeding like this. You are not behaving in a way that is safe for you, or for other drivers that are on the road." When he locked eyes with her she had to resist sticking out her tongue. She was normally a fan of Mitchell's but getting an actual speeding ticket from him when he could easily let it slide, left her feeling a little bitter.

Ida was more than a little annoyed as she glanced over her shoulder and then back in the other direction, further up the road.

"What other drivers?" she demanded as she glowered at him. "There's no one else on the road."

"Maybe not, but there could be," he said with certainty as he scribbled on the pad. "And what about that poor turtle?" he reminded her.

"He made it safely across the road," Ida spat back. "Is there some kind of turtle law I broke?"

"Ida, you have to understand, I'm doing this for your own good," Mitchell said frowning and finished filling out the ticket.

"You're not really going to write me a ticket, are you?" Ida gasped as she stared at him. "You can't be serious!"

"I'm quite serious," he replied and stepped closer to her. "You're putting yourself in danger, and I happen to like you," he explained as he ripped the ticket off the pad. "I also happen to know that Vicky and Sarah have warned you about driving recklessly. So, if you're not going to listen to them, then maybe you'll learn your lesson from having to pay this ticket."

"Unbelievable!" Ida huffed as she stared at him. "You're not going to get away with this, Sheriff McDonald will hear about this!"

"I'm sure he will," Mitchell frowned as he handed her the ticket. "But even if it means working extra shifts for a year, I wouldn't feel right if I didn't do something to try to get you to stop this dangerous behavior."

"Dangerous behavior," Ida muttered and shook her head. "You wouldn't know danger if it bit you on your toe!"

He raised an eyebrow and tried not to crack into a smile. Ida didn't notice the amusement in his gaze as she fretted. "I'm not paying this!" she added as she shoved the ticket into the pocket of her motorcycle jacket. "You can bet your fancy little hat that I'm going to fight this in court, and I'll win. This is harassment of the elderly," she added.

"Ida, you're not elderly," he reminded her and had to suppress a chuckle.

"I will be when I go to court to fight this ticket! I can play up to ten years older than I am, Mitchell. You're going to regret this, boy-o, yes you will! To think I used to like you!"

Mitchell shifted from one foot to the other and hoped that she couldn't tell that he was starting to actually get nervous. Ida was eccentric, but she was also very determined, and he had yet to see her not accomplish anything that she set her mind to.

"Ida honestly, I'm doing this for your safety..." he attempted to explain again.

"Lucky for you I don't have time to waste on arguing with you," she said harshly and fired up her motorcycle. "And don't you follow me either!"

As she peeled off down the road Mitchell stared in amazement. It wasn't so much Ida's behavior that stunned him. It was more how much she reminded him of Vicky that left him dazed.

***

Vicky glanced down at her phone to find a text from Mitchell indicating he had given her Aunt Ida a ticket for speeding. Vicky frowned with concern, not so much for the ticket, but for the fact that her aunt had been speeding. She was just about to step into Sarah's office to talk to her about it, when Ida burst into the lobby.

"Aunt Ida?" Vicky asked with surprise. "Are you okay?"

"I'm just fine, your ticket-giving boyfriend though, he has started a war he won't win," Ida wagged her finger with warning.

"Aunt Ida," Vicky began to say as she placed her hands on her hips. "You know he was only doing his job…"

"Never mind that," Ida said dismissively as she glanced around the lobby. "Where's Sarah? We need to talk," she walked over to the front desk.

"She's in her office, I think," Vicky said as she tucked her phone into her pocket. "What happened?" she asked curiously.

"Inside," she pointed to the office door and Vicky followed her inside. Once they were inside, Ida closed the door behind them. Sarah looked up from the papers she was reading over with surprise.

"We need to talk," Aunt Ida said sternly.

"Yes, we do," Sarah admitted as she laid the papers back down on the desk. "I just had a very unpleasant call from the Lambard family lawyer. The medical examiner confirmed that it was an allergic reaction and the lab tests proved that the food in the room was laced with peanut oil. This is not going to go away easily," she admitted.

"Well, I don't think it should," Ida said stubbornly. "But I do think that there is more going on here than meets the eye."

"What do you mean?" Vicky asked as she sat down across from Sarah's desk.

"While I was at the diner, I overheard Peter talking to one of the waitresses, Carolyn I think her name was," she explained. "She's his sister. It sounded to me like she was very happy to hear about Sandy's death."

"Wait, Carolyn? Are you sure?" Vicky asked as she studied her aunt closely.

"Yes, that's what he called her," Ida insisted. "The way they were talking, it sounded like Peter was the one who put the peanut oil on the food and she asked Peter if he had seen Gerald."

"When I was confirming some plans with Melissa about her bridal shower she said that Carolyn had thrown a fit over being invited to be a bridesmaid because she's involved with a married man," Vicky said thoughtfully. "I had no idea that Peter is her brother," she added. "Do you think they could have been talking about Gerald?"

"Slow down," Sarah requested with a shake of her head. "What are you suggesting? That Peter was not only involved but planned all of this?"

"It wasn't Henry," Vicky said passionately and stabbed her thumb against the surface of the desk in front of her. "Never in a million years will you get me to believe that Henry made a mistake like putting peanut oil into a bottle labeled sunflower oil and then put that oil on the food. So, it had to be someone else who had access to the kitchen."

"It wasn't Peter who planned it out either," Ida interjected. "From their conversation it seemed to me that it was Carolyn who had masterminded the whole thing."

"But what about Gerald?" Vicky suggested, her eyes wide. "Maybe he was involved, he just didn't lace the food. He had his lover, Carolyn, do it!"

"Wait, wait, wait!" Sarah smacked her hands firmly on the desk. "We're getting way ahead of ourselves. First of all, we don't know if Gerald was involved at all. From what you overheard, Aunt Ida, I understand why you suspect Carolyn and Peter, but we don't really know what they were talking about, and even if we did, we don't have any proof. If we go to the police and tell them that we suspect Peter, he is still our employee, and the inn will still be held responsible. If Peter did this I doubt that he will confess. We need to be very careful about our next steps. Let's sleep on this, and in the morning, we'll figure out what to do."

"Well, there's not much we can do tonight," Vicky agreed. "Let's meet up first thing in the morning. I really think if we bring Mitchell into this, he will help."

"Ha!" Ida snapped and rolled her eyes. "How? By giving us all tickets?"

"Aunt Ida, if you were speeding..." Sarah began.

"That's it, I'm out of here!" Aunt Ida declared and walked right out of Sarah's office.

"Aunt Ida," Vicky moaned and followed after her. "Mitchell was just trying to protect you."

"If everyone would stop trying to protect me, you all might just figure out that I am perfectly capable of taking care of myself," Ida flipped the collar of her jacket up and stalked off towards her room.

Once Ida was closed off in her room, and Sarah had gone home to get a break from the tension at the inn, Vicky stepped out onto the porch. A part of her hoped that Mitchell would stop by to join her, but she knew he was working. As she looked up at the stars that speckled the sky she thought about the events that had unfolded. She was so convinced that Henry was innocent, but she simply couldn't piece together how the peanut oil had ended up on the food. She closed her eyes and tried to go back through the day. She was sure that she must have forgotten about something.

Suddenly, Vicky recalled the shed door being open when she walked past it after she had cleaned up the pool area. She knew that was where all the peanut oil had been stored. Had Peter gone back out to the shed after all of the oil was put away? He was fairly new to the inn so he might not have known to shove the door shut.

Vicky swung slowly back and forth on the porch swing. It creaked quietly through the darkness that surrounded her. As she sorted through her thoughts she tried to recall everything about the day that had struck her as strange. It seemed so clear that Peter had been the one to put the peanut oil on the food. But she still had no way of proving it. As she closed her eyes she had to wonder, was Gerald involved? Did he play a bigger part in all of this than anyone realized?

Vicky knew that they had all agreed not to do anything else until morning, but she was impatient. She didn't want to give Gerald and Carolyn time to create cover stories or plant even more evidence to frame Henry or the inn. The inn was quiet with most of the guests having finished dinner and already settled into their rooms. It was a good time for Vicky to check in with Gerald. She knew he was still staying at the inn in a different room but she hadn't seen him since Sandy's death. As she walked back into the inn she caught sight of a figure near the corner of the porch. She turned to look, but didn't see anything more than the shadow of an old rocking chair. Shaking her head with annoyance she closed the door behind her.

Chapter Seven

When Vicky arrived at the room Gerald was staying in, she paused just outside it. She listened for a moment, hoping to be able to tell if Gerald was inside or not. While she was waiting for him to make some kind of noise she thought she heard footsteps. She turned around in search of the source of the sound. She didn't want other guests to catch her eavesdropping. But when she looked up and down the hallway there was no one to be seen. She drew a deep breath and reminded herself to be calm. She still hadn't heard a sound from inside the room. She lifted her hand to knock, but then she felt a little awkward. She didn't know how to broach the conversation with Gerald. It would seem odd for her to just show up at his room in the middle of the evening.

What if he was on the phone with Barry Baker? She decided she needed an excuse to speak to him. She walked down to the end of the hall where one of the maids' carts was sitting near a storage closet. She looked through it in search of something that would give her a good excuse to knock on his door. Then she found it. It was a fresh pile of towels. A guest could never have enough fresh towels. As she picked them up from the cart and began walking back towards Gerald's room she thought she heard a door click shut. But she didn't see anyone stepping out into the hallway. She paused in front of Gerald's door and then knocked on it sharply.

"Mr. Holstead?" she called out in what she hoped was a casual tone. She heard a scuffing sound, and then Gerald opened the door.

"Yes?" he asked with a hint of annoyance in his voice.

"I'm sorry to bother you, I just thought you might like to have some fresh towels," Vicky explained and shifted from one foot to the other as she tried to peer past him. His frame filled the doorway and left her little space for spying.

"At this time of night?" he asked skeptically. "Don't you have maids who do that?"

"Of course," Vicky nodded a little. "But we just want to make sure that you have everything you could possibly need. I noticed that the maid on your floor hadn't finished her rounds."

"Ah, I see," he smiled a little and accepted the towels. "You know a fresh pile of towels isn't going to change the fact that your chef's mistake killed my wife," he said bluntly and narrowed his eyes. Vicky hadn't been certain that Gerald was involved, but now she was really beginning to suspect him. His cruel tone and the pleasure he seemed to take in her squirming alerted her to the very real possibility that he was behind the plan to kill his wife.

"It's just a courtesy, Mr. Holstead," Vicky replied and attempted to keep her voice as even as possible.

"I understand," he nodded and then sighed heavily. "I'm sorry, it was rude of me to speak to you that way. I know this was all a terrible accident. I just still can't believe she's gone."

"Of course," Vicky said softly. "Perhaps there's someone I can call for you, a family member, or friend?" Vicky suggested hesitantly. "You shouldn't be alone at a time like this," Vicky pointed out.

"I'm afraid I'm not very popular with the in-laws," Gerald admitted with a slight shrug. "And I don't have family of my own. Sandy was all I had."

"I'm so sorry for your loss, Mr. Holstead," Vicky said as gingerly as she could. He seemed to be experiencing genuine grief, but she knew that some people were astoundingly good liars. From the grizzle that had grown up along his cheeks, and the dark circles under his eyes she was beginning to believe that he was truly lost in grief. "If there's anything I can do to help, please feel free to let me know," Vicky murmured softly.

"Thank you," Gerald nodded and turned away from the door. As he closed the door Vicky felt her heart drop. She had been so ready to accuse a man she knew very little about of murdering his wife. Now she was not sure what to think. She was starting to walk away when she heard a cry of surprise come from inside the room. She paused and turned back.

"What are you doing here?" she heard Gerald ask sharply. His voice was followed by a loud crash.

"What do you mean she was all you had?" a shrill voice challenged Gerald in return.

Vicky raised her hand to knock on the door, but before she could do so she heard Gerald's raised voice.

"You can't be here, don't you see how wrong it is for you to be here?" he demanded. Vicky decided not to knock. There was only one person who could be inside that room, and it sounded like Gerald hadn't been expecting her. When she pushed open the door the first thing she spotted was a lamp that had crashed to the floor and shattered. The next thing she saw was Gerald's pale face, and his eyes wide with shock.

"What's going on here?" Vicky asked as she stepped into the room. When she moved beside Gerald she finally saw Carolyn. She was standing in the center of the room with a large knife in her hand. Vicky immediately recognized it as a knife from the set in the kitchen. The knives were famous for being incredibly sharp. She started to step back out the door so she could call for help, but Carolyn jutted the knife towards Gerald.

"If you open that door you're going to be responsible for the death of both Holsteads," Carolyn warned with sheer fury in her voice. Vicky didn't think that Carolyn would actually hurt Gerald, but she couldn't take that risk. She remained where she was standing, her breath held as she waited to see what Carolyn would do next.

"Carolyn, I don't know what you're thinking, this is insane!" Gerald blurted out, he was obviously stunned, and more than a little frightened by the knife that Carolyn was holding.

"Insane?" Carolyn asked with a soft laugh under her voice. "What's insane about wanting to have what is rightfully mine?" she demanded. "The only insane thing about this whole situation is that you expected me to sit by and wait for years, years, to be with the man I love!"

Vicky's heart was racing as she saw the panic cross Gerald's features. What she didn't see was any sign of him feeling any affection for the woman who was wielding the knife.

"Enough of this," he growled and took a step forward. "I'm grieving, Carolyn, this isn't the right time for this discussion."

"You're grieving?" Carolyn giggled at that. "We should be celebrating! That's why I'm here," she smirked. "I knew that you wouldn't want to spend another night without me in your arms."

Gerald stared at her, absolutely astonished by what she was saying.

"Don't you know what's happened, Carolyn?" he asked with wide eyes. "Sandy is dead."

"Oh, she knows all right," Vicky volunteered boldly. She wanted Gerald to understand the level of danger he was in. "She's the one who planned this whole thing, aren't you, Carolyn?" Vicky asked.

"Oh hush, you're not even supposed to be here," Carolyn replied and then clenched her jaw to hold back some of her anger. "This is between myself and my fiancé."

"Fiancé?" Gerald gasped out as he took a step back from Carolyn.

"Don't you see, Gerald?" Carolyn smiled warmly, her eyes filled with an eager glow. "It doesn't have to be a secret anymore. We can tell the world the truth. Sure we'll have to put off the wedding for a few weeks out of respect for the deceased, but then we can make it official."

"Official?" Gerald repeated in a distant voice. It was clear that he wasn't keeping up with Carolyn's words.

"Sure, Carolyn decided she couldn't wait anymore for you to decide to leave your wife," Vicky supplied, which drew another glare from Carolyn. Vicky was trying to gauge just what Carolyn's intentions were, and how she was going to react when Gerald didn't respond to her the way that she wanted him to.

"I need you to listen closely to me, Carolyn," Gerald said as calmly as he could. "You're talking like a crazy person. Just put down the knife, and we can figure all of this out."

"There's nothing to figure out," Carolyn spat back. "My brother took care of what you weren't brave enough to accomplish yourself. He wanted to make sure that I was taken care of, and now I will be."

Gerald made a strangling noise inside his throat as he finally realized what Carolyn was admitting to.

"What have you done, Carolyn?" he asked, his voice trembling as he stared at the woman pointing the large butcher knife at him.

"Oh, don't act so innocent, just because someone else is listening," Carolyn said dismissively. "You knew exactly what I intended to do," Carolyn growled in return, her eyes darting from him, to Vicky, who was standing as close to the door as possible.

"I didn't know!" Gerald insisted, his voice rose as he spoke vehemently.

"You did! I told you I'd find a way for us to be together, and this is how I did it," Carolyn growled fiercely.

"I didn't mean this!" Gerald groaned as fresh tears filled his eyes. "I never meant this, Carolyn."

"What did you mean?" Carolyn demanded as she stared at him with growing intensity. "Were you lying to me when you said that you wanted to spend the rest of your life with me?"

Gerald stared at Carolyn for a long moment. Vicky realized that Gerald had an important choice to make. If he was honest with Carolyn she might just attack him with the knife. Gerald seemed to come to the same conclusion she did.

"I wasn't lying," he said quietly. "But I didn't want it to happen like this, Carolyn, not like this," he gasped out and stretched out his hand palm up before him. "Give me the knife, Carolyn, we can't let this get any worse. Let me help you," he pleaded as he tried to meet her eyes. For just a moment it looked as if Carolyn might falter, her expression softened, she lowered the knife slightly. Vicky held her breath, hoping that the situation would be over before it could escalate further. But an instant later a hardness arose in Carolyn's eyes. She glared at Gerald and lifted the knife once more.

"Shut up!" Carolyn demanded with frustration. "I did this for you. I did this because you promised me we would be together."

"In time!" Gerald shouted back, obviously beginning to lose control of his emotions as he glared at her. "I asked you to be patient. I came here to see you, to be with you. I convinced

Sandy to spend our vacation here just so that I could sneak in some time with you. I risked everything to show you how important you are to me, and this is what you did behind my back?" he shook his head with disgust. "This never should have happened."

"I did what you weren't brave enough to do," Carolyn spat in return. "I had to. It was the only way for you to be free."

"Free?" he asked with rage growing in his voice. "You made me a suspect in my own wife's death, Carolyn! How do you think it looked when I was standing there with an empty EpiPen? How is that free?"

"Why did you even pick it up?" Carolyn hissed. "I made sure that Peter emptied it out. All you had to do was sit there, and watch her die!"

"I couldn't do that," Gerald breathed out, his body beginning to shake. "She was a person, Carolyn..."

"She was in our way!" Carolyn roared and shoved over another lamp beside her.

"Now, look where we are," Gerald gulped out and hung his head. "Now, look at this mess," he uttered in a defeated whisper.

"That's because of her!" Carolyn hissed and spun the knife in Vicky's direction. "All she had to do was stay out if it! But no, she had to find out the truth, she had to be sneaky. She was in the diner today asking about me. If she had just left things alone..."

Vicky tensed as she felt Carolyn's fury focus on her. She knew that she meant nothing to Carolyn, it would be easy for the woman to take her rage out on her.

"I just wanted to find out the truth," Vicky protested as she flattened herself against the door. "Henry didn't deserve to take the fall for something he didn't do."

"Oh, that's right, let's talk about who deserved what," Carolyn huffed. "As if Sandy deserved all that money just for being born into the right family, as if she deserved Gerald just because she was beautiful. No, that's not how this world works," she growled. "I couldn't sit back and wait to get what I deserved, I had to reach out and take it!"

Vicky noticed that Carolyn was steadily creeping closer to her.

"Carolyn, I didn't do anything to stop you," Vicky whispered breathlessly.

"You did everything," Carolyn hissed as she glared at her. "You stirred things up, when they should have all fallen into place. Now you're going to pay for that!" she growled as she began to hurl herself towards Vicky. Vicky slid out from in front of the door just as the door opened. The opening door struck Carolyn in the side and sent her stumbling a few feet back as Aunt Ida pushed her way into the room.

"Vicky! I just found out that someone spotted Carolyn on the property!" Ida proclaimed as she barreled through the door of the room, nearly knocking Vicky to her knees. Carolyn jumped back a few feet to gain her bearings, and Ida tensed when she saw the knife. Ida released the door and it swung shut.

"Yes. I'm aware of that," Vicky said through gritted teeth as she slowly stood back up. Carolyn was glaring between Ida and Vicky, while Gerald was still trying to catch Carolyn's eyes.

"Carolyn please, this is getting out of control," Gerald pleaded as he took a hesitant step closer to her. "There's nothing we can do to change things now, but you shouldn't be making this worse. Let these women go, they have nothing to do with this," he attempted to reason with her, his tone as gentle as it could be.

"They have everything to do with it," Carolyn spat back with increasing frustration. She used the knife to emphasize her point, stabbing the air with each word she spoke. "Why is that so hard for you to understand? They ruined everything! We were supposed to get married, now how can we do that?" she demanded.

"They didn't ruin it," he replied sharply. "Carolyn, you've lost sight of reality. I never wanted Sandy dead!"

"How could you not?" Carolyn argued back, the knife swinging wildly through the air. "She was the only thing standing in the way of our love. Now, you will inherit her fortune and we will be able to marry," she moved closer to Gerald the knife still held firmly in her hand. "Isn't that what you want, too?" she asked desperately as she looked up into his eyes. "Gerald?" she whispered his name shakily.

Gerald swallowed thickly as Vicky and Ida stood close to one another. The way they were positioned meant that they could not get to Carolyn without directly confronting the blade that she was wielding.

"We're going to have to distract her," Ida whispered to Vicky who nodded.

"And before she figures out that Gerald isn't going to marry her after all of this," Vicky whispered back to her. She glanced around the room for something she could use to distract Carolyn.

"That's right, Carolyn," Gerald whispered soothingly as he held her gaze. "Now, we can be together. Now, we can have our whole future together. But, we can't do that if you are in jail, can we?" he murmured and held out his hand, palm up. "Give me the knife, sweetheart, just give it to me and this can all be over."

"No," Carolyn shook her head slowly back and forth. "It won't be over until all of the witnesses are dead," she whispered to Gerald. "You have to help me, I can't get to them both."

"Carolyn," Gerald exhaled in wonder and shock.

"The sunflowers," Vicky whispered to Ida. "If I can get a hold of the vase I can splash the water in her face."

"If you can splash the water in her face, then I can get that knife out of her hand!" Ida promised as she bent her knees slightly and positioned herself in an attack stance.

"Are you sure?" Vicky asked nervously as she studied her aunt. "I don't want you to get hurt."

"Listen, if we don't get that knife out of her hand, then someone is going to get hurt!" Ida hissed in her direction without looking at her. Vicky nodded a little, she knew that her aunt was right, and if anyone could disarm Carolyn it would be Ida. The trick was getting to the vase of sunflowers without Carolyn noticing.

"Are you going to help me or not?" Carolyn asked Gerald. "I killed for you, are you willing to do the same for me?" Carolyn held his gaze.

"No," Gerald breathed out as he stared at her incredulously. "No, I won't kill anyone, Carolyn, can you even hear yourself? What you're saying?"

"Are you saying you don't want to marry me?" Carolyn demanded as she glared at Gerald. "I did this, all of this, for you!"

Gerald moved towards her very cautiously, blocking Vicky and Ida from Carolyn's view.

Vicky knew that this was her opportunity. This was the moment that could mean the difference between Gerald living and dying, not to mention ensuring their own safety. She lunged for the vase. She felt her hands close around it and was spinning back towards Carolyn with it when there was a loud pounding on the door. The sound was so loud that it made everyone in the room jump. Vicky almost dropped the vase she was holding in her hands. She felt the room sway around her as panic threatened to overwhelm her. The pounding came again and Carolyn raised her knife in the air.

"If I can't have you, then no one will!" she announced loudly as she prepared to plummet the knife into Gerald's chest.

"I'm looking for Ida," a booming voice declared through the door of the room just before it was forced open. Carolyn tensed and looked towards the door, halting the downward movement of the knife. In that moment Vicky splashed the water from the vase in the direction of Carolyn's face. The sunflowers hit her face and then fell to the floor and the water hit its mark. Carolyn shrieked in surprise. She took a few steps back but still gripped the knife tightly in her hand.

"What's going on in here?" Rex demanded when he stepped through the door and saw the scene unfolding. Vicky had dropped the vase on the floor, causing a loud crash. In the same moment Ida launched herself forward in the direction of Carolyn who was still trying to blink water out of her eyes.

"Ida!" Rex cried out as Ida slammed her body into Carolyn's waist, and took the woman down to the floor with her. Carolyn landed with a hard thump on the floor. Gerald bolted out of the room as Vicky started to move towards her aunt's side. Carolyn still hadn't let go of the knife.

"Gerald!" she screamed out as she fought with Ida over the knife. Vicky was trying to find a way to help her aunt, when Carolyn managed to wriggle her wrist out of Ida's grasp. Vicky's heart felt as if it had come to a complete stop when the knife arched through the air and glistened in the overhead light as it began to swing back down. Before it could, Rex had shoved her hand to the floor. He pinned it and the knife down to the floor with the sole of his black steel-toed boot.

"Stay down," he growled as Ida pinned Carolyn's other arm. Vicky quickly grabbed one of the blankets off the bed to use as make-shift handcuffs. She could already hear the sirens in the parking lot and assumed that Gerald had called the police. She stared down at Carolyn, writhing, crying, and screaming Gerald's name. She felt her heart sink as she recalled the defeat in Sandy's eyes when she described the perfume she had smelled on her husband's clothing. She had thought she was only losing a spouse, she had no idea that she was going to lose her life as well. She had a fortune at her disposal, but there was no amount of money that could protect her from the jealousy of an unbalanced woman in love.

"It wasn't supposed to be like this," Carolyn whined as the room flooded with officers. Vicky was relieved to see that Mitchell was one of them.

"Vicky, are you hurt?" he asked as he rushed to her side. Rex and Ida stood back as Carolyn was flipped over and handcuffed. The knife was collected for evidence.

"I'm okay," Vicky assured him as she rested her head lightly against his chest. Feeling his arms around her was exactly what she needed after witnessing such an encounter.

"Are you sure?" he murmured beside her ear as he held her.

"I'm sure," she sighed as she looked over at Ida and Rex. Rex had looped his arm around Ida's waist. She was leaning on him and clinging to his hand. It was a sweet and vulnerable moment that Vicky had rarely seen her aunt display. "Rex arrived just in time," she added and slowly shook her head.

"Can you tell me if Gerald was involved?" Mitchell asked quickly. "He's claiming he wasn't."

"He wasn't," Vicky shook her head. "At least not in Sandy's death, in breaking her heart, yes, he was very involved. But no, this was something that Carolyn and Peter did together."

"How sad," Mitchell frowned and gave her another light hug.

"I know, I know," Vicky sighed. "You have to go."

He smiled sadly and nodded. Vicky watched as he took the lead on the investigation. As she walked to the window of the room and looked out over the employees' quarters she saw most of the staff standing outside. Henry was standing nervously outside his room. She met his eyes through the window and smiled. He nodded in return and finally breathed a sigh of relief.

Chapter Eight

That Sunday was the bridal shower. How quickly the town forgot about the scandal that had arisen overnight and seemed to pass just as quickly. Everyone was ready to celebrate Melissa's future marriage, and her bridesmaids were thrilled to have an afternoon to frolic through the inn and the grounds. Vicky glanced over the south garden which faced the sun for the longest period of the day. The gardener was planting a fresh patch of flowers, in honor of Sandy and her family.

The Lambard family dropped its investigation into the inn's liability concerning Sandy's death. As Gerald had admitted to infidelity he was not entitled to any inheritance due to a specific clause in Sandy's will. Carolyn and Peter were behind bars and would be for several years to come.

There was a certain sense of closure that filled the inn and made it possible for the staff and guests to move on with their lives. Sandy's murder had been solved and her murderer had been held accountable. Joy had returned to the Heavenly Highland Inn, most aptly reflected in the shrill giggling of a group of happy twenty year old women.

Vicky was glad that the shower was such a success. The games, the food, and the companionship had all come together very well, and it was just what the inn needed to have a fresh start. Just what Vicky needed, was a patrol car pulling up in the parking lot of the inn as she walked across the gardens. She paused and smiled as she watched the car door open and Mitchell step out. She was surprised that he was no longer in his uniform, but he looked just as handsome. As he walked towards her she felt a familiar thrill at how lucky she was.

"Hey, there," he called out as he walked up to her. "I hope you don't mind me crashing your party."

"No, I don't mind at all," she smiled in return and leaned up to kiss him softly on the lips. "I'm so glad to see you."

"Not nearly as glad as I am to see you," he grinned. "Do you think I can join in on some of the festivities?" he inquired as he watched one of the bridesmaids streak across the lush grass with a toilet paper train sticking to the back of her dress.

"Oh, of course, there's always room for one more," Vicky laughed out loud at the thought of Mitchell participating in the 'catching the bouquet' practice that was coming up next. "But I'm not ready to share you just yet," she murmured and sighed as he wrapped his arms around her.

They looked at Melissa excitedly grasping a bouquet of sunflowers that Vicky had arranged, using flowers from the garden.

"She better be careful, she is suffocating the sunflowers holding that bouquet so tightly," Mitchell laughed.

"I know," Vicky giggled. "She is just so excited."

"A lot has happened over the past few days," Mitchell whispered. "I'm sorry I wasn't around more to support you while it was happening."

"You were around," she smiled and kissed his cheek. "You made sure Aunt Ida was safe," she reminded him with a glimmer in her eye.

"Yes, I think I'm still going to pay for that," he laughed at that as Ida glowered at him from beside the pool where she and Rex were having an afternoon in the sun.

"I just wish all of this hadn't happened," Vicky admitted with a sigh.

"It's terrible that someone's jealousy had to lead to such a tragedy," Mitchell shook his head as he watched the women happily sample the cake.

"It is," Vicky agreed as she recalled Sandy's certainty that Gerald had been having an affair. She had been right to suspect him, but he wasn't the most dangerous person in her life. "You know, after the way he spoke to Carolyn, I almost believe that he really wasn't ever going to leave Sandy, and not just because of her money. He seemed heartbroken that Sandy was dead."

"Perhaps he realized what he had far too late," Mitchell suggested as he brushed a strand of Vicky's hair back from her eyes.

"All I know for sure is that the inn isn't going to be held responsible, even though the peanut oil was found on the food. Peter has confessed to going into the shed, refilling the bottle with peanut oil, and adding the fatal dose to the food before the meals were delivered," Vicky sighed and took Mitchell's hands in her own. "So, Henry's job is safe as well. Now, if only we can do something about your job," she smiled a little.

"Well, I hope I'm finally back in Sheriff McDonald's good graces. He was not exactly impressed with the voicemail that Ida left on his phone, but he did say that anyone who dared to write her a ticket was impressive," he grimaced a little. "We'll see how long that lasts."

"Well, I think Aunt Ida is going to be a little busy with her new beau," Vicky grinned. "Hopefully she won't give you too hard a time."

"So, Ida didn't mind a little protection after all?" Mitchell asked with a light smile as he wrapped his arms around Vicky's waist.

"I guess it just had to be the right hero coming to her rescue," she smiled warmly and leaned up to kiss his cheek. "We all need just the right hero."

"So, should I dismiss the ticket?" he asked as he met her eyes.

"Not a chance!" Vicky laughed out loud and shook her head. "I wouldn't miss out on witnessing the scene she's going to put on in that court room, for anything!"

"You do realize that I'm going to have to be there too, right?" Mitchell asked with a soft chuckle.

"Which is exactly why you're my hero," Vicky grinned and kissed him gently.

As they both pulled back from the kiss a cheer went up from the women who were gathered around the lace-covered tables in the middle of the gardens.

"Sounds like someone else is a hero, too," Mitchell chuckled as he watched Sarah beam in response to Melissa's happy shrieks as she opened the envelope and read the card explaining that the inn was going to host her wedding for free.

"Sounds like the inn is going to have some more good memories to look back on," Vicky smiled as they walked towards the tables together. "Oh, and by the way, at the wedding, I already have a dance partner," Vicky smiled happily.

"What?" Mitchell pretended to be shocked. "I'm going to miss out on bruised toes?"

"Henry is going to teach me to be graceful," Vicky smiled.

"Ah well, there's the real hero of the day then," Mitchell laughed loudly and ran off across the grass as Vicky chased after him.

The End

More Cozy Mysteries by Cindy Bell

Heavenly Highland Inn Cozy Mystery Series

Murdering the Roses

Dead in the Daisies

Killing the Carnations

Drowning the Daffodils

Bekki the Beautician Cozy Mystery Series

Hairspray and Homicide

A Dyed Blonde and a Dead Body

Mascara and Murder

Pageant and Poison

Conditioner and a Corpse

Makeup, Mistletoe and Murder

Hairpin, Hair Dryer and Homicide

Blush, a Bride and Body

Shampoo and a Stiff

Printed in Great Britain
by Amazon